No Time for Regrets

Heartlines

Books by Pam Lyons

A Boy Called Simon
He Was Bad
It Could Never Be
Latchkey Girl
Danny's Girl
Odd Girl Out
Ms Perfect

Books by Anita Eires

Tug Of Love
Summer Awakening
Spanish Exchange
Star Dreamer
Californian Summer
If Only . . .
Teacher's Pet
Working Girl

Books by Mary Hooper

Love Emma XXX
Follow That Dream
My Cousin Angie
Happy Ever After
Opposites Attract
A Love Like Yours
Heartlines Stories

Books by Barbara Jacobs

Two Times Two

Books by Jane Pitt

Loretta Rose
Autumn Always Comes
Stony Limits
Rainbows For Sale
Pia
The Boy Who Was Magic

Books by Ann de Gale

Island Encounter
Hands Off

Books by Anthea Cohen

Dangerous Love

Books by David S Williams

Give Me Back My Pride
Forgive and Forget
My Life to Live

Books by Jill Young

Change of Heart
Three Summers On

Books by Ann Ruffell

Friends for Keeps
Secret Passion
Baby Face

Books by Lorna Read

Images
The Name is Zero

Books by Jane Butterworth

Spotlight On Sam

Books by John Harvey

Wild Love
Last Summer, First Love

Books by Anita Davies

Stepsisters

Heartlines

David S. Williams

No Time for Regrets

A Pan Original

First published 1987 by Pan Books Ltd,
Cavaye Place, London SW10 9PG
9 8 7 6 5 4 3 2 1

ISBN 0 330 29931 X

Printed and bound in Great Britain by
Richard Clay Ltd, Bungay, Suffolk

Chapter 1

Mrs Grainger clapped her hands together. The sound reverberated through the silence of the school's gymnasium which had for the last five weeks served as the 'O' level examination room.

'Right! Put down your pens, please.'

Her imperious voice echoed round the long bare room, its floor protected by a thick canvas covering. She stood just in front of me, tall and slim in a light blue suit, still young-looking in spite of being well into her forties. She clapped her hands again, quelling the growing murmur.

'Don't leave until you're told.' Her words had the authority of a typical headmistress as she glanced around to make sure that not one of us was cheating. 'I want all your answer papers collected first.'

I sat back in my chair, sighed and yawned and rubbed my aching eyes. It was all over. I'd sat my last exam and it was all over.

Tomorrow would be my first day of freedom – and wasn't I going to make the most of it!

Since my name was Alison Anderson, mine was the first on the register and therefore I'd been placed in the first desk near the entrance to the changing rooms. I glanced round at Kate Howard, my best friend, seated about five desks back and gave her a grin as I rolled my eyes. She did the same in return and mouthed some words I didn't understand.

Then a minute or two later, Mrs Grainger told us we could all leave. There was a scrape of chairs and a frantic rush for the door followed. Seconds later, I was out in the sunlight of a late June afternoon, breathing in the fresh air. Not that you could really call it fresh. I lived in Grimborough, an aptly named small town in the Midlands; a town I hated and couldn't wait to get away from. Where had once been green fields and woodlands, there were now acres and acres of houses and small factories. The air was thick with car exhaust and the incessant drone of heavy traffic.

I stood aside from the others and waited for Kate to catch up. We had been friends since our earliest days in primary school and were so alike with dark hair cut short that we were often mistaken for sisters.

'What did you think of it?' She fell in beside me and together we ambled across the school yard.

'Not a lot!' I grimaced. 'But then, geography never was my best subject. Think you've passed?'

'Me? I doubt it.' We arrived at the dual carriageway that ran in a semicircle around the perimeter of the school campus and climbed the metal bridge that connected it to the town. 'Anyway, who cares? I don't really need geog. to get into the Tech . . . '

That was true enough. Both Kate and I had already decided to become nurses and had opted for the pre-nursing course at the local technical college.

We reached the small shopping centre which was where our ways parted, but it was also the home of the 'Bacon Butty', a small café which was a favourite haunt of most of the fifth formers.

'What about a coffee?' I suggested. 'To celebrate our freedom!'

Kate gave a grin. 'Why not! I don't fancy going home yet. I want to unwind first.'

I led the way into a rectangular restaurant where we ordered coffees and, in honour of the occasion, Danish pastries.

'Do you realize, Alison, it's all over? No more going back to Grimborough Comp. ever ever again. I can't believe it.'

'Nor me.' I confessed. 'I'll just have to keep my fingers crossed that I get the right grades to get into Tech . . . I don't know what I'll do if I don't . . . '

'Don't be ridiculous. Of course you'll get them. You've worked hard enough . . . we both have.' Kate grinned mischievously. 'If you don't, you won't meet that handsome doctor you've set your heart on, will you?'

'Can I help it if I want to get away from Grimborough?' I said loftily. 'What girl in her right mind would want to stay here?'

'Oh, Alison. It isn't as bad as all that . . . '

'Not that bad!' I exclaimed. 'How can you possibly say that? It must be one of the grottiest towns in England . . . '

'Come off it. I know it's not very pretty . . . '

'You've noticed . . . . '

' . . . and it wouldn't be everyone's favourite town . . . '

'You can say that again.'

' . . . but it's got a lot going for it.'

'Such as?'

'Well . . . ' Kate puckered her forehead. 'It's got a good shopping centre . . . and Birmingham's not far away if you can't find what you want around here . . . '

'True. But London has even better shops . . . '

Kate just ignored my interruption. 'And there's the lido. It's got one of the best swimming-pools in the whole of the Midlands. You know it has.'

There was no denying that. Grimborough boasted an Olympic-sized swimming-pool in the centre of town with a swimming club – of which both of us were members. In fact, I lived for swimming; it was my favourite sport, and though it sounds like boasting, I was good at it. My room at home was festooned with trophies – at least my side of it was. The other side, where my thirteen-year-old kid sister Julie slept, was a jumble.

'And of course there are all your friends.'

Kate had the uncanny knack of being able to make me feel guilty by mentioning the most simple of things.

I shuffled uncomfortably. 'Leaving Grimborough wouldn't mean I'd lose touch with all my friends,' I protested, 'especially you – I'd never do that.'

'Not even when you marry this glamorous doctor who's just waiting for you . . . though he doesn't know it yet.' She took a sip of coffee and shook her head gravely. 'I must say I feel sorry for him. If I knew who he was, I'd warn him . . . '

I gave her my sweetest smile. 'Thanks, Kate. Who needs enemies when there are friends like you about?'

But she wasn't put off by my sarcasm. If anything, it only provoked her to further comment.

'And of course there's Phil.'

I felt my cheeks begin to burn. 'What about him?' I muttered.

'Well . . . he is your boyfriend. Or had you forgotten?'

I hadn't forgotten. 'He's all right,' I began.

'All right?' It was Kate's turn to show her annoyance. 'He's a good-looking guy – and you know it . . . '

'That's true. But . . . '

'But nothing, Alison Anderson. If you ask me you don't know when you're well off.'

'Well, nobody's asking you,' I said, standing up. 'Anyhow, just because we're going steady right now doesn't mean we'll get married one day . . . ' I paused and added, ' . . . any more than you'll marry Kenny . . . '

Kate was stung by my comment. She was crazy about Kenny Robertson.

Seeing her so hurt made me regret my words.

'Oh, Kate. You know I didn't mean that,' I said gently. 'I'm sure you and Kenny'll get married. I think you're made for each other. It's just . . . oh, I don't know . . . I'm just not sure about Phil and me, that's all . . . '

She followed me out of the 'Bacon Butty' and walked silently along the main road.

'Did you really mean that about Kenny and me?' she asked. 'Do you really think we're made for each other?'

'Of course I do,' I replied. 'I wouldn't say it if I didn't, would I?'

A minute later, we parted, agreeing to meet later at the swimming club. As I ambled off towards home, I couldn't help thinking about Phil. I'd known him for as long as I'd known Kate, which might be part of the trouble. But like Kate had said, he was a nice guy . . . good-looking too. Perhaps it was tied up with wanting to get away from Grimborough and becoming a nurse because I seemed to know instinctively that when I did, it would all be over between Phil and me.

When I arrived home my sister Julie was quarrelling with Paul, my nine-year-old brother (as usual), and my mother, who was in the kitchen preparing dinner, was yelling at them. I felt my stomach plunge as I heard their shouts; lately, the perpetual squabbles were getting on my nerves.

As I walked into the long narrow room, the air smelling deliciously of steak and kidney pie, my mother turned and gave a loud sigh of relief.

'Thank goodness you've arrived,' she said. 'Find out what's wrong with those two, would you, darling? I'm trying to get dinner ready . . and your father's trying to sleep in the lounge . . '.

I rushed up the stairs and stormed into the bedroom to find Julie sitting in front of the dressing-table, putting on some lipstick. Paul was perched on my bed, glowering at her.

'What on earth's going on?' I demanded. 'You've heard Mum shout up at you.'

Paul looked up, his moist, blue eyes appealing to me.

'She hit me,' he complained. 'For nothing . . . '

Julie turned angrily. 'Liar!' she snapped. 'I was putting on my make-up and you bumped me . . . deliberately'.

'No, I didn't!'

'Oh, yes you did. You came up behind me and pushed me . . . '

'Didn't!'

The quarrel was starting all over again.

'Stop it!' I ordered. 'You know very well that Dad is trying to sleep . . . he was up early this morning and if you wake him, you know what you'll get . . . '

As if on cue, a voice shouted up from the bottom of the stairs. 'Will you two stop shouting.' It was Dad, his voice still muzzy with sleep. 'If I have to come up there . . . '

'Now you've done it!' I whispered urgently. 'If he does come up, you know what you'll get. Come on Paul, go to your own room before you two really get into trouble.'

Reluctantly, he slouched out, leaving me alone with Julie. She and Paul were always quarrelling and though he could never be called an angel, Julie wasn't exactly innocent either. In fact, lately I found her a pest myself, and it really got me down to have to share a bedroom with her. I longed for privacy – a room I could call my very own and retreat to whenever I wanted.

'I hope you'll clear up that mess,' I said, nodding at the mass of tissues crumpled in a heap on the floor. 'And you know Mum doesn't like you using make-up.'

She looked at me in the mirror and grimaced. 'You going to tell her then?'

'No, I'm not. I'm just warning you. Just let her catch you with it on, that's all . . . '

I returned downstairs to help Mum with the meal. When I thought about it, that was another reason for getting away from Grimborough. I needed a room of my own where I could do just as I wanted without having a kid sister around making life difficult.

I joined Mum in the kitchen and as I stood watching her I realized just how well we got on. Suddenly I felt guilty about wanting to leave so desperately. I knew we'd both miss each other.

'How did the exam go?' she asked, taking some cutlery from the drawer and handing it to me.

'All right!' I gave an apathetic shrug. 'I managed to answer most of the questions . . . '

'Well that's something, isn't it? With a bit of luck, you'll get the right grades and go to the Tech in September, won't you?'

'I'll need more than a bit of luck – I'll need buckets full . . . '

She gave me a hug. 'Not to worry, love. I know you've done your best, and that's all your father and I expect. All you can do now is wait and forget all about it for the time being.'

She was right. It was exactly what I intended to do. Put it all behind me and enjoy the summer holidays. But though I didn't know it then, before the end of those holidays I was going to learn many truths about myself, and my life was going to have more than its share of happiness – as well as pain.

Chapter 2

'Well, Alison. Now you've left the Comp., what are you going to do with all the time you've got on your hands?'

We had finished dinner and Dad, Mum and I were sitting in the living room. Julie had gone to our bedroom – probably to practise applying her make-up again – while Paul had left with some of his friends to play soccer in the park.

'After all,' Dad went on, 'you've got almost three months before you start at the Tech.'

'I'm not sure. I've applied for a temporary job in Tesco's but I don't think they'll take me on. Some of the girls at school said the vacancies were all filled.'

Dad gave one of his slow grins. 'It'll give you more time to practise your swimming,' he said, stretching his legs out in front of him. 'Bob Jarman reckons you'll make an excellent swimmer one day . . . '

Bob Jarman was the coach in charge of the town's swimming club and had represented England in several international events.

My father's revelation made me feel warm and excited. 'Did he really say that? Honestly?'

'Of course. I met him in town the other day and he told me how well you were progressing.'

Mum rolled her eyes in mock despair. 'Honestly,

Jack. You and your swimming. Why can't you leave the girl alone?'

'But, Mum!' I protested. 'I like swimming. and if Mr Jarman says I'm good, it's important . . . '

'I thought that nursing was important, too.'

'It is, but so is swimming. There's nothing to say I can't enjoy both, is there?'

Mum didn't reply. But Dad hadn't finished.

'Did he say when he'd be taking the club to the lakes again?'

Bob Jarman was dead keen on long-distance swimming, and as soon as I was sixteen he had taken me to Witham Water, a large lake about twenty miles north of town. I'd taken to it like a fish to water – literally.

I shook my head. 'He did say he might go in a couple of weeks.' Dad nodded with satisfaction. 'Good. If you give me enough notice I'll try to arrange a day off and drive you there.'

Dad was a shift engineer at one of the local factories, and had once been a good swimmer himself. It was mainly because of working awkward hours that he'd given up swimming seriously. Mum often thought that he encouraged my swimming just for his own satisfaction, but that wasn't true. I liked swimming, especially now that I'd discovered I was good at long distances.

Dad and I got on really great and having him watch me swim – and encourage me – made me feel proud.

'I'll ask him tonight if you like,' I said.

I left just before seven with my duffel bag thrown carelessly over my shoulder, and hurried to the leisure centre where Kate was already waiting. As I entered the large modern building the pungent smell of chlorine greeted me, and though I was quite used to it by now, it still provoked a strange feeling of excitement – just as it had all those years ago when my father had first taught me to swim. I don't think I was more than four at the time.

Hurriedly, I changed and paddled through the foot-bath to the edge of the pool where for one brief moment I paused at the side. Then I took a deep breath and launched myself into the water. I felt the coldness flow over me, making me shudder as I glided inches beneath the surface. My body quickly adjusted to the temperature, and when I rose to the surface I broke into a front crawl, my favourite stroke. Soon I had adjusted my breathing to my stroke, and I was ploughing effortlessly through the water. I wasn't all that good at sprinting, but I really enjoyed swimming slowly, taking my time and revelling in the tranquillizing activity. That was why I liked long distances so much; though it was tiring, I found it soothing too. It was as though I were in a dream world and my body in a state of weightlessness.

Then I became aware that Kate was by my side, keeping pace with me. We must have swum at least ten lengths – about half a mile – before I heard a whistle blow and knew that Mr Jarman had arrived. I swam the last few yards, touched the smooth tiles and with one easy movement, heaved myself on to the side. Seconds later, Kate joined me and for a few moments we sat breathlessly together, the water dripping off our heads and trickling down our backs.

Then Mr Jarman called to us.

'Right, you two – the Terrible Twins. Over here at once, if not sooner.'

We grinned and padded over to where he was sitting on one of the low slatted benches that circled the pool. Around him were other members of the swimming club, about twenty in all. 'I'm glad you're all here,' he said when we reached him, 'because I wanted to speak to you before we got down to training.' He put a hand into his pocket and brought out a letter. 'I had this earlier this week. It's an invitation for eight members of our club to attend a course – a residential course in Wales . . . anyone interested?' He glanced around and grinned with pleasure when he saw our response.

'I thought you might be. As a matter of fact, we're lucky to be invited this late. I reckon some other club must have dropped out at the last minute.'

'Where's it held?' I asked.

'A place called Castell Brenin,' he answered. 'It's a residential sixth form college, something like Gordonstoun, you know – the place Prince Charles went to . . . only not quite so famous. And the swimming-pool has to be seen to be believed.'

'Will we be the only ones there?' It was Kate this time.

Mr Jarman gave a laugh and shook his head. 'Hardly! There'll be clubs from all over the country.'

One of the other members, a guy called Steve Lawson, asked when it was going to be held and how much it would cost.

'The second week in July – that's in two weeks' time – and as for the cost . . . ' He scratched his head. 'I'm afraid it's going to be rather expensive. Over a hundred pounds.'

I felt my heart sink and there was a groan from the others.

'But,' he continued, 'the club is prepared to subsidize you. As a matter of fact, it will only cost you just over fifty pounds. As well as the cost of getting there, of course.'

He glanced around at us all. 'But like I said, there are only eight places, so we may have to put your names in a hat and pick out the lucky ones.' He paused. 'Well? How many are interested?'

I was certainly interested, especially as I knew I could manage the fifty pounds. I had more than that saved in my bank account and I was sure that Dad would approve of my using it in this way, even if Mum might frown. Besides, since I had now finished school, there was nothing to stop me.

Then I remembered the job I'd applied for. What if Tesco's offered me one in the next few days? I dismissed it from my mind. Going on a course like this was decidedly more important.

I looked at Kate. 'How do you feel about it?'

She didn't hesitate. 'I'm going. Nothing's going to stop me. It's the chance of a lifetime.'

That decided me. Along with almost everybody else, I put my name forward.

We spent the rest of the evening going through our programme, until just before half past nine when Mr Jarman announced it was time to finish and asked all those interested in going to Castell Brenin to gather round.

'I've put your names on separate pieces of paper,' he explained, holding up an old hat that must have belonged to a tramp. 'Does anyone want to check them?' Since no one doubted his word, he went on. 'Very well. Perhaps someone will pick out the first name. How about you, Alison?'

He held the hat up high, and dipping in my fingers, I drew out the first of eight folded papers. Mr Jarman opened it and read out the name.

'Kate Howard,' he announced. 'Congratulations, Kate. Now it's your turn.'

Kate picked out Steve Lawson's name, and then Steve pulled out Glen Drew's. And so it went on until there was just one place left. My name was still in the hat along with a dozen others, and I felt my stomach twist with apprehension when I realized just how bad the odds were against me. I knew I wouldn't be going. I just knew.

'Now for the last one,' said Mr Jarman.

I held my breath as he unfolded the small strip of paper, silently read it, and looked up. I felt my heart thump deep inside me as I waited.

'The last place goes to . . . ' He paused and grinned, deliberately prolonging the agony. ' . . . Alison Anderson!'

I put my hands to my mouth to quell a scream of delight, while Kate jumped and hugged me.

'But don't forget,' he said to each of us as we went to the changing rooms. 'I'd like your deposits in by next week and the remainder the following Friday.'

We were still in a state of excitement as we made our way to the coffee bar on the ground floor. Phil and Kenny were already there, and before we had even sat down, Phil was at the counter ordering our drinks. He was about three inches or more taller than I was, muscular, with light brown hair and a rugged sort of charm.

Why then, I asked myself as I watched him return, did I feel about him as I did? Lots of girls would have given the earth to go out with him. Why didn't I care one way or the other?

He grinned as he placed two steaming mugs of coffee in front of us.

'Have a good swim?'

I nodded. 'And heard some exciting news,' I replied.

I told him about the course and my enthusiasm was so great that it was only when I finished that I realized how quiet he was.

'In two weeks . . . two weeks tomorrow, as a matter of fact.'

'I see.'

His disappointment was now too obvious to ignore, and I had the sudden niggling feeling that I had forgotten something that I shouldn't have.

Then I remembered. Phil had already arranged for us to go to Birmingham for the day. 'Oh, Phil!' I exclaimed. 'I'd forgotten all about our trip together.'

He shrugged his shoulders. 'It's all right. I understand . . . '

What it really meant was that some things – swimming for instance – were more important than him, and it made me feel guilty.

'I've promised Mr Jarman now . . . I've put my name on the list . . . ' I was searching desperately for excuses. 'I can't let him down, can I?'

I glanced at Kate and saw the embarrassment in her eyes; she knew that all I had to do was tell Mr Jarman I couldn't go. Others would jump at the chance to take my place. I felt my cheeks burn.

'Forget it!' Phil said lightly, and gave a tight-lipped

smile that hid his true feelings. 'It's important that you go on that course. You couldn't possibly turn it down. I wouldn't let you anyhow.'

I put my hand on top of his and gave it a squeeze.

'Thanks, Phil!' I said, my voice full of selfish relief. 'I knew you'd understand. We'll go to Birmingham another time.'

Phil nodded. 'Yeah. Why not?' he said.

We left shortly afterwards and stopped at a take-away to share pasties and chips. Phil was subdued and I knew that he was still disappointed about not taking me to Birmingham. Yet there was something else there too.

He kissed me briefly at the gate and waited for me to go into the house before walking away. I waved and when I closed the door behind me, I leaned against it wishing with all my heart that I could feel differently about him.

But things were yet to happen which would make me realize just how good a friend he was.

Chapter 3

Phil's behaviour really got me down over the next two weeks; he became so moody and possessive that I wanted to scream. I should have known how he was going to be right from the very start because that following night, he hardly let me out of sight at the disco. And when he found me dancing with another guy, I thought he was going to explode.

It was ridiculous really. He'd been at the bar for ages and judging by the queue that he'd joined I knew he was going to be some time. Kate and Kenny were smooching to a slow number while I was left on my own, with nothing to do but watch. Then this guy came up and asked me to dance.

Knowing the mood Phil was in, I was about to refuse when I realized it was Jason Stokes. Jason was a couple of years older than me and had once lived a few doors away, until his parents had moved to a quiet area a mile or two out of town. I hadn't seen him in years.

'Didn't recognize me, did you?' he said with a grin as he took me on to the floor. 'Go on! Admit it!'

It was the same old Jason Stokes, full of mischief and even better looking than he had been as a kid, with dark wavy hair that flopped over a broad tanned fore-head. His eyes still twinkled. He had always managed to make me laugh, just as he made me laugh now.

'If you must know,' I replied. 'I didn't. You've changed . . . '

He smiled down at me. 'For the better, I hope.'

'Well . . . ' I began and looked at him closely. 'You've grown, haven't you? You weren't so tall when I last saw you.'

'True!'

'And you're different.'

'So are you. You were pretty enough when we lived in Rugby Road. You're even prettier now . . . '

His words made me blush with pleasure and before long we were talking about old times like long-lost friends, which we were in a way, and I almost forgot about Phil.

But then Jason said, 'You don't happen to be on your own, do you? Because if you are, you could join us. Me, Sheila and Graham I mean.'

'Sheila and Graham?'

'Sheila's my girlfriend and Graham's her brother. He's home on leave from the Army and on his own . . . ' I shook my head. 'Sorry, Jason. I'm with my fella.'

'That's a shame. I think you'd have liked Graham.'

At that moment, the dance came to an end and he walked me back to my table. Phil was already there and I introduced them to each other. Phil was very polite – too polite perhaps – and though he didn't say anything, I could tell that he hadn't liked me dancing with Jason, which wasn't like Phil at all.

He was off-hand all evening, and when we danced I could feel his tension.

In the end I couldn't stand it any longer. He had been silent all the way home and when we reached the porch, I turned to him.

'Come on, Phil. What's wrong with you tonight?' I demanded. 'What's bugging you?'

He shuffled uncomfortably. 'I don't know what you mean!'

'Oh, yes you do.' I wasn't going to let him off the hook so easily. 'You've hardly spoken to me all evening.'

I waited for him to reply, but all he did was look down at the floor.

'You didn't like me dancing with Jason, did you?'

He looked up, his eyes indignant. 'Of course I didn't mind . . . '

'Come off it, Phil. Do you think I'm stupid or something? I could sense it the minute I came off the floor.'

He shook his head. 'You're wrong. I didn't mind you dancing with him. Why should I?'

'Then what is it?'

He looked up. 'Do you really want to know?'

'Of course I want to know,' I cried in exasperation. 'I wouldn't ask you if I didn't.'

He took a deep breath. 'It's you, you've changed . . . You're different . . . I don't know where I stand with you any more. I'm just not sure of you . . . that's all.'

I sighed at the irony of it all. I was too sure of him, and he wasn't in the least sure of me. Where was it all going to lead us?

I had a phone call the following Tuesday which reminded me that I hadn't asked Mr Jarman when we would next be going to Witham Water. It was Mr Jarman himself informing me that he had hurriedly arranged a swim for the following day.

'I have a day off work,' he explained, 'so I phoned up Steve Lawson and a couple of the others to see if they could manage it. How are you fixed?'

I told him that it was fine with me and when he suggested picking me up at ten thirty the following morning, I asked him to hold on for a moment while I asked my father.

Dad was mowing the lawn at the time, and when I told him of the arrangements, he nodded enthusiastically.

'Tell him I'll drive you there,' he said, and added with a grin, 'I'll do anything to get out of doing the gardening.'

So it was arranged that we'd meet Mr Jarman and the others at the lakeside shortly after eleven.

It was a beautiful morning as Dad drove out of town, and half an hour later we were in the heart of the countryside, passing through several sleepy villages until we arrived at the small gravelled car park on the edge of the lake. The sun was shining strongly on my back as I stood at the edge, gazing at the far bank. The water was clear and bright; I could see the pebbles under it for several feet until the land shelved steeply and they disappeared into the dark depths. I shivered involuntarily, wondering what lay down there; big fish, pike, goodness knows what. I had to shake myself free of my vivid imagination.

Dad put a hand on my shoulder.

'You've got a nice day for it,' he commented. 'Not a trace of a breeze to disturb the surface, though I must admit the water looks cold.' He bent down and put his hand in. 'I'm right. You're going to need a good covering of lanolin today. Come on, let's give you a hand putting it on. The others should be here soon.'

There was a brick-built changing area near the car park, complete with showers, and when I returned in my speedo swimsuit, I found that the others had arrived. There were two cars and a large white van which carried several canoes and a dinghy.

Mr Jarman came over while the others unloaded them. It was the rule that for each swimmer there was a canoeist to act as a safety man in case of cramp or exhaustion, as well as a dinghy with outboard motor to rescue anyone in trouble. He and Dad exchanged greetings while I went over to the others. I discovered that Glen Drew, who had decided not to swim that day, was going to be my canoeist.

'Don't do anything stupid,' he advised, as he

humped his canoe down to the lake. 'If you get tired or feel your muscles seizing up, give me a yell. I'll only be a couple of yards away.'

I gave him an appreciative smile. All the men were safety conscious, perhaps even more so because I was so young, and a girl as well – though that part of it made me mildly annoyed; after all, I was a much better swimmer than most boys my age. So why should they treat me differently?

Dad was right about the water; it was freezing, as I discovered as soon as I put my big toe in. Glen had already pushed his canoe out and was waiting a few yards away, his head turned to watch me as I hobbled over the pebbles. As soon as the water reached my thighs, I adjusted my cap and goggles and launched out. I gave a loud gasp and shuddered as the water covered my shoulders, so much so that Glen laughed. 'Rather you than me,' he yelled.

I didn't yell back. I couldn't. My teeth were chattering so much that they were actually tapping a frantic Morse code – probably an S.O.S. which everybody ignored. But I remembered Dad's advice: once you're in, keep going and don't stop, especially at the beginning. Build up your body heat, develop a regular rhythm and you'll be okay.

It wasn't as simple as that, but I took his advice and before long, I willed myself to ignore the cold. Glen and Mr Jarman took me around the edge of the lake, not because they lacked confidence in me, but because Mr Jarman wanted to cover a longer distance. I concentrated on maintaining an even stroke, and thought of anything and everything in an effort to keep monotony at bay. At one point, I felt like giving up and it was only

Mr Jarman's encouragement that kept me going.

It was just over two hours later that we arrived back at the point where we'd started to discover my father waiting with a watch in his hand.

He threw a towel over my shoulders as I padded out, shivering in spite of the sunshine, and thrust a cup of hot coffee into my trembling hands.

'That was good,' he congratulated me as I sipped the warming drink. 'You must have swum at least four miles . . . and in good time . . . '

Mr Jarman nodded. 'This girl of yours is going to go far, believe me . . . '

But I was shivering so much, I could hardly thank him for his kind remarks. I hurried to the changing room and spent at least ten minutes under a soothing shower until all the lanolin had been washed away and my body was warm again. Then I returned to the car to munch a crusty ham roll.

Half an hour later, it was time to return home.

'See you on Friday,' Mr Jarman said as we completed the task of loading the canoes into the van. 'I've already had confirmation from Castell Brenin. They're looking forward to seeing us.'

As we drove away, I waved goodbye to Glen Drew. I thought excitedly of the course and felt my stomach tighten with eager anticipation.

The following Friday when we took our deposits to Mr Jarman, he gave us details of the arrangements he had made. 'I've hired a minibus to take us there,' he explained, 'and the club committee has agreed to pay for the hire as long as we chip in for the petrol. How do you feel about that?'

There was a murmur of approval.

'Good!' He went on, 'All we have to do now is agree on a time to leave, remembering that we're expected at Castell Brenin for dinner. That means we should leave here soon after lunch.'

'How long will it take us to get there?' someone asked.

Mr Jarman scratched his head. 'I've checked the distance on the map and I reckon it's about 150 miles, give or take a mile or two, so if we manage to average forty miles an hour, it should take about four hours. I think we should leave at one. That gives us some leeway if I get lost. Remember! This driver . . . ' He jabbed his chest with his thumb, ' . . . has never been to "Wild Wales" in his life.'

There were no other questions so it was agreed that we should meet outside the leisure centre the following Saturday afternoon at one o'clock sharp.

'Right then.' Mr Jarman clapped his hands and rubbed them together. 'Let's get on with our training, shall we? I don't want the other clubs showing us up. Believe me, you're going to meet some excellent swimmers when you get there, and make some very close friends,' he added.

His words made my skin break out in goose pimples and I had the sudden feeling that he had seen into the future and that soon my life would be changed in a way which was going to surprise and delight me.

Chapter 4

It was eight days later when we set out for Castell Brenin. I had packed my suitcase the previous night, but had decided to buy a new swimming costume. Kate had mentioned casually as we walked around town that there would probably be several boys on the course, and since my present swimming costume was looking rather worn, I thought it wise to get a new one. After all, I didn't want to appear a shapeless hulk at the pool-side.

As soon as I'd had breakfast, I hurried to the sports shop in town. It didn't take me long to decide which costume to buy: an Arena Super Freeback Lycra costume in navy with a cream trim. Then as I was leaving, I saw one with navy and gold wavy stripes on a white background that looked fantastic, so on impulse I bought it instead. I had spent more than I'd intended, but as Kate had said, you never know who you might meet on these courses.

Mum drove Kate and me to the leisure centre shortly after half past twelve. Though we were the first there, within ten minutes all eight of us were ready to leave. But just as Mr Jarman was packing the last suitcase on to one of the spare seats, Phil came cycling up.

'Hoped I'd catch you,' he said breathlessly. 'Wanted to wave you off . . . and to give you these.'

He handed me a box of chocolates.

'Oh, Phil,' I said, touched by his kindness. 'You

shouldn't have.'

He shrugged his shoulders and grinned. 'It's nothing much. Just something to eat on the way.'

Then Mr Jarman tapped me on my shoulder. 'I hate to come between two love-birds, but if we don't leave soon, we'll be late getting there.'

Phil gripped my hand and squeezed it. 'Enjoy yourself,' he said and gave me a gentle smile. 'See you when you get back.'

Tears pricked my eyes as I got on the bus. Phil was a great guy; I'd never known anyone kinder. But something was missing, and I didn't know whether it was my fault or his, or whether we were both to blame.

Then Kate spoke. 'You don't know when you're well off, Alison Anderson. Not only does your fella come to wave you off, but he buys you boxes of chocolates as well.'

I sat back and sighed. She was so right.

Then she nudged me. 'Don't sit there dreaming. Open the box and let's see what they're like.'

As Mr Jarman had predicted, the journey was long and tedious. We travelled along the M6 motorway for about half an hour, joined the M5, and within three quarters of an hour we could see Wales. The mountains loomed black in the distance as we left the motorway and meandered along quiet country roads, climbing higher and higher into the hills. The scenery was fantastic; bare windswept mountain tops, rugged and grand, with views that stretched for miles, while below us, the sides of the valleys were carpeted with trees.

'Not far now,' Mr Jarman called to us. 'Just twenty

miles or so . . . shouldn't take us long.'

He was being optimistic and hadn't allowed for the twists and turns of the road, so it was an hour later before we went through a small village called Cwm Brenin. It boasted a pub, a post office, a small church and two streets of stone-built houses. Then we followed a sign which announced that Castell Brenin College was just half a mile away.

Castell Brenin College was surrounded by a high stone wall and the entrance was flanked by two large pillars on which were hung tall, wrought iron gates. Our bus rattled over a cattle grid and followed a gravelled drive lined with shrubs and trees. After a hundred yards or so, the college came suddenly into view: a large stone building with a crenellated top, mullioned windows and rectangular Elizabethan chimneys. In front of the main door, the drive ended in a circle, in the centre of which was a lawn. We came to a halt and Mr Jarman turned and said, 'Well, we're here. Hold on a minute and I'll find out where we have to go.'

Kate and I were so excited we couldn't stay on the minibus a minute longer, but before we could wander far, Mr Jarman returned with a youngish man dressed in a light blue track suit.

'This is Mr Keen,' he announced. 'He's the gentleman in charge of the course.' We all nodded and murmured our welcome. 'If you get your suitcases, he'll show you the way to your rooms.'

Mr Keen waited as Mr Jarman unloaded our cases.

'This your first time here?' he asked Kate and me. He had fair hair and the strong muscular shoulders and slim hips of a swimmer. 'I'm sure you're going to enjoy it. The training's hard but we have plenty of fun too.'

By this time, our cases were in our hands.

'Right! If you follow me,' he went on, 'living quarters are to the rear of the Old House.'

He led us into a foyer and through a maze of corridors until we emerged on to a covered terrace. We were in a quadrangle of cobbled stones with one large building in front of us, which was clearly the gymnasium, and two smaller buildings to the right and left.

Mr Keen nodded to the building on the left. 'Ladies' bedrooms are over there; gents' on the opposite side.' At that moment, a young woman came out of the gymnasium.

'Jan!' Mr Keen called. 'Could you come here for a moment, please?'

As she came over, he said, 'Jan Webster is one of our coaches and is here if any of you young ladies need any advice. Jan, would you take these girls to their room, please? They're in D16.'

She was slim and pretty with light brown hair tied back in a pony tail. She gave us a welcoming smile.

'Sure. Come this way.'

We followed her across the quad to the door in the centre of the dormitory block and up a flight of stairs to a room on the second floor. She talked as we went, telling us the times of our meals and what we would be doing during the following week. Then she opened the door and stood aside.

It was a surprisingly large room with two single beds, two study tables and a large old-fashioned wardrobe. There were two casement windows with small panes which faced out over the quad.

'You're lucky,' Jan Webster said. 'This is one of the

best rooms in Glendower House. During term time, it belongs to the senior councillors – that's what we call our prefects.' She glanced at her watch. 'Mr Keen's arranged a welcoming meeting at six o'clock in the gymnasium and that will be followed by dinner in the refectory.' She glanced around. 'Now, if there's nothing you'd like to ask me, I'd better meet the others.'

I threw myself on to my bed. 'Isn't it fantastic, Kate!' I sighed. 'Much better than our school . . . '

Kate slung her case on to her bed and started to unpack. 'I should hope so. We paid to come here, remember.'

Trust Kate to be so practical. I wondered as I looked at her if she was as excited as I was. If so, she gave no sign of it.

'You're not going to lie there all night, are you?' she said, glancing round as she hung her clothes in the wardrobe. 'You've got less than half an hour until the welcome . . . and I don't know about you, but I'm going to wear my newest gear. After all, there must be some unsuspecting males somewhere waiting to meet us . . . '

That stirred me out of my reverie, and within ten minutes I'd unpacked and was ready to go down. By this time, we could hear others arriving, their excited voices carrying down the long corridor as they were allocated their rooms. Feeling as nervous as two abandoned kittens, we made our way to the gymnasium.

My stomach was churning as I followed Kate inside and smelt the tang of polished wood. Mr. Jarman waved to us from the bench on which he was sitting and we joined him, adding to the excited murmur of voices. I glanced around at the other members of the course. Most of them were my age and most of them were girls, which didn't make me feel too happy. Two girls to every boy meant the competition was going to be twice as fierce – and I didn't mean at swimming.

Kate had been thinking the same thing. 'There aren't many guys, are there?' she whispered.

'Aren't there?'

She glanced at me, disbelief evident in her eyes. 'Don't tell me you haven't noticed!'

I shook my head innocently. 'As a matter of fact, I haven't.'

Her frown darkened. 'Alison Anderson. You're a liar.'

'And you're boy mad,' I replied. 'We've come here to practise swimming, remember. Not chase guys . . . '

She gave me one of her sweetly malicious smiles. 'Sorry, Alison. I'd forgotten. Thanks for reminding me.'

Then she nudged me with her shoulder and sent me sprawling on to the floor.

'Oh, sorry, Alison!' she said, her voice full of mock concern. 'I seem to be doing – and saying – all the wrong things, don't I?'

At that moment, Mr Keen came in with Jan Webster and half a dozen other coaches. He leaned against the wall bars, welcomed us and introduced us to all the officials.

'I'm afraid not everyone has arrived yet. We've been waiting for the party from Beckhaven to turn up. Anyhow, I don't think we can wait any longer, so I might as well begin: Training starts at seven thirty,' he said to a chorus of friendly groans, 'followed by breakfast at nine thirty. Then there's an hour's rest period . . . ' Cheers greeted this. 'Then weight training in the gym.' Groans.

So he continued, until he had covered the programme. Then he called out our names, allocating us to our personal coaches.

'There may be variations from day to day,' he concluded, 'but that's your normal programme. And if there are any changes, your coach will let you know. And now, I think dinner should be ready. Oh! And one last thing. After dinner, we'll take you all on a tour of the college. Meet your coach in the quad at eight o'clock.'

He led us out to the refectory, a long hall with low beams and a highly polished floor, with long oak tables which reminded me of a public school dining hall. There were no tablecloths, just place mats ringed with cutlery. I sat facing the coaches' table with the door at its side.

Then Mr Keen rose to his feet. 'Would you stand, please?' After the shuffling had stopped he said a prayer in Latin. He looked up. 'Thank you', he said and sat down.

It was all so strange and new. I hadn't said grace before a meal since junior school, and never in Latin.

The food was served by maids in black dresses and white aprons, and though in a way it was like having school meals all over again, the food, though plain, was much better cooked. I glanced around as I ate, occasionally joining in the friendly conversation, and noticed the empty places opposite us.

'Must be for the people from Beckhaven,' I mused to

myself, popping a piece of bread into my mouth. 'I wonder what they're like. Hope they're all boys.'

Almost in answer to my prayer, the swing doors opened and a tight cluster of boys came in. But I only had eyes for one of them. He was tall, broad shouldered, with dark brown wavy hair, and so good-looking that I couldn't help gasping.

And suddenly I knew!

Chapter 5

Of course, I had bread in my mouth and it went down the wrong way, so that I coughed and spluttered until my eyes watered.

Then a voice asked, 'Everything all right?'

I looked up and saw a beautiful face looking at me from the opposite side of the table. It was the guy who had caused the problem, making every nerve in my body tingle.

'I'm Jeremy Sinclair,' he said as he sat down. 'I'm with the Beckhaven party.' Kate jumped in and replied before I could get my breath back.

'I'm Kate Howard,' she said cheerfully – and cheerfully I could have strangled her. 'And this is Alison Anderson. We come from Grimborough.'

'That's in the Midlands, isn't it?'

By this time, I'd recovered from my fit of coughing. 'That's right. Have you ever been there?' and when he shook his head, went on. 'Lucky you! You don't know what you've missed!'

He was joined by another guy who squeezed on to the bench. 'This is Damien,' Jeremy said in introduction. He had straight fair hair and light blue eyes. 'Damien Masterson. He says he's my best friend, though you wouldn't believe it sometimes.'

We all laughed and I breathed a sigh of relief because Damien soon made it apparent that he was interested in Kate. The four of us got on marvellously during dinner and by the time we had finished our sweet, I was convinced that we were going to become more than good friends.

Jeremy got to his feet. 'We've got to go and unpack. Did I hear right? Have they laid on a disco for us later?'

I nodded. 'That's right. But there's a tour of the college first. Eight o'clock in the quad.'

He glanced at his watch and frowned. 'We'll have to hurry if we're going to make it. If not, see you at the disco.'

Then he and Damien left and I wondered if he was merely being polite. After all, just because I had met him first didn't mean I had any rights over him. By the time he got to the disco he could quite easily have met someone else far more attractive than I was. Already I had noticed several girls further along the table glance in his direction with the look I knew only too well.

Then Kate nudged me. 'We'd better hurry too if we're going on that tour. We've just enough time to get ready.'

Back in our room I thought I'd find out what Kate thought of Jeremy and Damien.

'What did you think of them?' I asked, being deliberately casual, as though I couldn't care one way or the other.

She was applying her make-up at the dressing-table mirror. 'Those two at the table? All right, I suppose. I thought Jeremy was rather dishy.'

You would, I thought. 'Damien was nice-looking.' It was just as well to point out his strong characteristics too, I decided.

Kate pouted her lips and glanced at me in the mirror. 'Yes . . . he was all right. Nowhere near as nice as Jeremy though. Now he's the sort of guy I could really fall for.'

Oh, great! Now there were two of us after the same guy, and that spelt trouble. But my face must have shown what I was thinking because Kate suddenly burst out laughing.

'What's wrong with you?' I demanded, suddenly suspicious.

All Kate could do for a moment was shake her head. Then she wiped her eyes with the back of her hand.

'You – that's what's wrong!'

'Me? What do you mean?'

'It's obvious, isn't it? You've been dying for me to tell you that I don't fancy Jeremy.' A giggle burst from her lips. 'Oh, Alison, you're so funny. Of course, I don't fancy him. I much prefer Damien.'

She'd been stringing me along all the time, deliberately making me jealous.

'Thank you very much, Kate Howard.' 'Just you wait . . . I'll get my own back on you!'

Then the very devil entered into me. I picked up her lipstick and calmly painted a crooked line right down her nose. She looked at me in sheer horror. 'Alison!' she screamed. 'Why did you do that? Now I'll never get down to the quad in time.'

'That's right,' I smiled sweetly. 'And if you don't, you'll miss the chance of teaming up with Damien, won't you?'

I've never seen Kate move so fast in all my life. Within two minutes she had removed the offending streak and had caught me up before I was half-way down the stairs. But as for teaming up with Jeremy and Damien, we were both in for a bitter disappointment. Though Mr Keen waited five minutes for any late-comers, neither of them arrived for the conducted tour of the campus.

Not that it took long. Within half an hour it was all over. We were first shown around the old castle, which wasn't really a castle at all, we discovered, but an Elizabethan fortified manor house. It was all very interesting, except that I was more anxious to know where Jeremy might be, and kept glancing over my shoulder in case he should suddenly appear.

Mr Keen then led us through the main lecture rooms to the gymnasium and playing fields, and to a large lake at the foot of the hill. It was all so impressive, but the swimming-pool was the highlight of the tour, with its range of equipment including a video camera and underwater observation panels.

'As you can appreciate,' said Mr Keen as we all trudged up the gentle slope to the college, 'all this costs money, which is why it's so expensive to come here, and why the college authorities let out the place during the summer vacations.'

I was suddenly aware just how lucky I was. It really

was the chance of a lifetime, just as Mr Jarman had stressed. But it made me envious to think that some people were lucky enough to live here all the year round, while all I had was grotty old Grimborough.

And then, to cap it all, as we came back past the junior common-room, we discovered Jeremy and Damien sitting around one of the coffee tables, chatting up two other girls.

Honestly! I wanted to cry. Why had I bothered to go on that stupid tour? Kate felt as miserable as I did. We both sat gloomily in our room gazing at each other without saying a word, until at last, Kate said with a sigh, 'Well, Alison. It's not much use sitting around here all evening. We might as well go down to the disco. You never know, we might meet two other guys . . . just as nice.'

She said it without much enthusiasm – and even less conviction.

'What other guys?' I said moodily. I knew deep in my heart that I wasn't going to meet another guy like Jeremy – ever.

But the sound of the music wafting up from the common-room persuaded us that we couldn't lie on our beds all evening. I couldn't have gone to sleep with the throb of music drumming in my ears even if I'd wanted to. Perhaps Kate was right. I swung my legs off the bed.

'Come on then!' I said with resignation in my voice. 'It's your idea. Let's go and see who else we can find.'

Everyone else must have arrived before us because they all seemed to be enjoying themselves, and though the flashing lights usually lifted my spirits even when I was feeling at my moodiest, they did nothing for me that night. Kate and I edged ourselves past the small group around the door, and crept unwillingly into the large room. The low tables and armchairs had been moved to the sides and at one end a small bar had been opened selling soft drinks, crisps and chocolate biscuits. Yuk!

I felt so isolated, my disappointment at not seeing Jeremy there making me feel despondent and laconic. Kate and I danced together, hardly noticing what we were doing, just looking down at the floor.

This is great! I kept thinking. Fantastic! What more could any girl want? Dancing with her best friend.

Then a hand tapped me on my shoulder and a voice spoke.

'Hey! Where have you been all evening? I've been looking everywhere for you!'

In spite of the din, I recognized that voice. My heart gave a sudden leap and began to soar. It was Jeremy. And when I turned to face him, I gave him one of my most dazzling smiles.

'Damien and I have been keeping a place for you at our table,' he explained, bending closer so that I could hear him. 'We were just beginning to give you up for lost.'

At that moment, the music came to an abrupt end, and the disc jockey began to announce the next record, but I wasn't listening. I just let Jeremy lead me to the table and only then did I realize that Kate had been willingly abducted by Damien. As I sat down next to him, I thought back to our talk in the room. If we hadn't decided to go down when we did, we'd have missed them completely. And they'd have teamed up with two other girls instead. The thought made me go cold.

The rest of the evening flew – which wasn't surprising, seeing that the disco came to an abrupt end at eleven o'clock.

'Sorry, everybody,' Mr Keen announced. 'This is where it all ends for tonight. We've got an early start in the morning. And believe me, you're going to need all the sleep you can get.'

But I didn't need any sleep, not at that moment, so when Jeremy suggested going for a walk around the grounds, I didn't hesitate.

We walked past the gymnasium and wandered along a winding path through clumps of rhododendron bushes until we came to a bench overlooking the lake. A moon had risen, a huge moon that dominated a dark velvet sky and dimmed even the brightest star.

Jeremy told me all about himself, about the small seaside town where he lived, about how his mother was the local doctor while his father owned one of the large stores in the town. I could have gone on listening to him all night.

'What about you?' he asked at last. 'What's your town like?'

My heart sank just to think of it. I shrugged my shoulders. 'Oh . . . ' I tried to think of words to describe it. ' . . . it's grotty. It really is. Just roads and houses and factories . . . and absolutely flat . . . not a hill to be seen anywhere . . . '

Jeremy laughed at the despondency in my voice. 'Come off it. It can't be as bad as all that.'

'It is! It's worse. I hate it there.'

There was a moment's pause as if my anger had disturbed him.

'Of course,' I went on, 'the people can be nice – sometimes.'

I thought suddenly of Phil, a recollection that made me feel so guilty that I swiftly thrust it out of my mind.

'But it's nice here, isn't it?' I continued quickly.

'Yeah! It's great!' he said, and as he looked into my eyes, he added, 'And the people here are nice too.'

His head came closer and for a moment I thought he was going to kiss me. But he suddenly glanced at his watch.

'Hey, look at the time!'

I felt my stomach twist with disappointment, but the next minute he took my hand in his and smoothed away all my disappointment.

'Come on,' he said softly. 'Let's walk back.'

We ambled slowly up the hill until we came to my dormitory block.

'See you in the morning,' he said. 'Shall we have breakfast together?'

I nodded. 'I'd like that,' I replied and opened the door. 'Till the morning then.'

I floated up the stairs and into my room to discover Kate already in bed.

'Ho, ho!' she said mischievously, her eyes glinting with amusement. 'Where have you been? And who with? As if I need to ask.'

I flung myself on to my bed and gazed dreamily at the ceiling.

'Oh, Kate!' I sighed happily. 'A couple of hours ago I thought everything was awful, and now . . . '

But Kate didn't want to listen to my romantic ramblings.

'And now perhaps we can all go to sleep,' she said in her usual matter-of-fact way.

With that, she put out the light and left me to undress in the dark. But I didn't mind. I knew I was going to enjoy the coming week even more than I'd expected.

Chapter 6

I dropped off to sleep that night dreaming of Jeremy, and when I awoke next morning, he was the first person I thought of. Even though it was half past six, I jumped out of bed and flung open the curtains. Kate groaned and pulled the sheet over her head.

'What time is it?' she muttered, her voice muffled under the bedclothes.

'Half past six,' I replied, standing by the window and looking out over the valley. A soft morning mist hugged the banks of the lake.

'Half past six!' Kate made no attempt to get out of bed. 'What did you wake me up at this time for?'

'Because we have to be at the pool by half past seven.' I walked over to her bed and pulled the clothes away.

Kate gave a scream and pulled them back. 'That was a horrible thing to do,' she complained and promptly disappeared.

Once more I pulled the blankets away, but this time she was prepared. She clung to them, holding them to her chin and glared at me.

'I don't need a whole hour to get ready,' she announced. 'Ten minutes will be long enough.'

Her indignation made me laugh. 'But it's too nice to stay in bed,' I said. 'Come on! Let's go for a walk down to the lake!'

She looked at me as though I had lost my sanity. 'Alison Anderson! Meeting that guy last night has driven you mad. If you want to walk there half way through the night, I'm not going to stop you. But if you expect me to accompany you, you'd better think again.'

Then she pulled the bedclothes over her head and snuggled down.

'Oh, well!' I sighed. 'If you want to waste your life, that's up to you. But if Jeremy and Damien are up early too, and some other girl happens to pluck Damien away from you, you'll have no one to blame but yourself. After all, the early bird catches the worm.'

A hand plucked a corner of the bedclothes and pulled it down. A malevolent eye appeared, squinting up at me.

'So that's what you think he is? A worm. Just wait until I see him. I'm sure he'll be delighted to hear the news.'

Then the bedclothes were pulled up with a final flourish and I didn't see her again until we met at the pool.

I washed and dressed and within a quarter of an hour, was seated on the bench where we'd stopped the first evening, though now in the cold light of day, it seemed as though it had all been a dream. In a way, that's just what it was and I wondered how it was going to end.

I didn't see Jeremy until we all assembled at the pool-side. I'd put on my new costume and as he came towards me I couldn't help noticing his appreciative glance. We spoke for a while until Mr Keen came in and called for silence.

'As you know, I've already placed you in your groups, but I thought I'd better remind you. I'd like you to stay in these groups for the rest of the week because, as you'll notice, I've put all the freestylers together, the same for those who specialize in the breaststroke, the butterfly, and so on. Each group will be coached by an expert in that particular stroke, so with a bit of luck you'll all be champions by the end of the week.' There was laughter at this, and then he added, 'If you could add a pinch of talent and a lot of hard work to that luck, you'll make me very happy indeed.'

Then he called out the names of the students in each group again, and it was with more than a twinge of excitement and delight that I discovered that Kate, Damien, Jeremy and I were together.

The next two hours were spent in the usual regime: stretching exercises at the pool-side, followed by twenty lengths warming up, then four lengths of the front crawl, backstroke and breaststroke, as well as kick and pull exercises when we used the floats and pull-buoys. Once that was over, Mr Keen and Jan Webster, who were our coaches, concentrated on the front crawl. By the end of ninety minutes when they called us on to the pool-side, we were absolutely shattered.

We had breakfast and then went to lounge in the common-room for the hour rest period. Jeremy joined us and asked if I'd like to come down to the village.

'I want to get some stamps. I promised my mother I'd write as soon as I got here, and you know what mothers are like,' he said with a mischievous grin.

I didn't have to be asked twice and together we strolled down a road so narrow that at times, the branches of the trees touched overhead and formed a tunnel of green light.

Now that I saw it properly, Cwm Brenin was even smaller than I'd thought. You could have walked past without realizing it: just a church with a small triangular patch of grass outside the gate, a pub called the Brenin Arms, a post office and general store, and perhaps a dozen houses at the most.

The post office sold everything from stamps to sausages, as well as sweets and ice creams, and we emerged licking thick wafers.

Jeremy nodded at the pub opposite, 'Must call there one evening. Fancy coming?'

'Yes, please!' I replied, not bothering now to hide my enthusiasm or my pleasure. The time for being coy had long passed.

He grinned at me, making my heart beat faster and my stomach churn and turn cartwheels.

'Great!' He took my hand and squeezed it. 'D'you know, Alison. I think I'm going to enjoy myself this week, I really do . . . '

I smiled back fondly. 'So do I!' And silently said to myself, 'I already am.'

We ambled back up the hillside through the tunnel of leaves, where he put his arm around my waist, and arrived back at Castell Brenin just in time for the next session – an hour's bout of circuit training in the gym. That was one activity I never truly enjoyed, but with Jeremy a few yards away and the prospect of being even closer to him when we'd finished, I actually found myself happy to do as Jan Webster ordered.

The rest of the day passed in a haze of gruelling training sessions and when they finally called time, I thought my arms would never move again. Limply I made my way to the common-room and flopped into an armchair. Cocoa and sandwiches had been provided and Jeremy looked at them with an expression of disgust.

'I'm starving,' he protested. 'I want something more substantial than this.' Then he leaned forward and whispered conspiratorially, 'Listen you three. What about going down to the village? There's a pub there that serves bar meals.'

Kate began to say, 'But Mr Keen said . . . '

Until my elbow met her ribs. 'Who cares what Mr Keen said! We don't have to do exactly as he says, do we? I mean, no one actually checks up on us. We could go wherever we please.'

'As long as we're back by eleven,' Kate reminded me needlessly. 'They close the doors then.'

'So they close the doors at eleven,' I said with impatience. 'We'll just have to make sure we're back before then, won't we?'

Jeremy was grinning. 'Well? What do you say?'

'I'm with you,' I said, with Damien coming a close second.

We all looked at Kate. 'Oh, all right!' she said with a sigh of resignation. 'I know when I'm beaten!'

But once inside she started again 'Your mother would hit the roof if she knew you were drinking lager, and so would mine,' she said in a whisper so loud that I felt sure they could hear.

I leaned forward. 'Keep your voice down, can't you? What are they going to say if they hear you talking like a kid just out of school? I'm only going to have one. One lager can't hurt you . . . '

'All right then!' she replied officiously. 'Just remember to keep it to one.'

But how could a girl of sixteen possibly do that? We'd finished our drinks by the time our food arrived, and since Jeremy and Damien had paid for it, it seemed the most natural thing in the world to buy the next round.

Kate wasn't happy and she showed it. But to my relief, she made no protest. She sipped her second glass of lager quietly, though I couldn't help noticing that when we left she had only drunk half of it.

Feeling giggly and reckless the three of us didn't really care about getting back, but Kate's obvious concern urged us on. Everything seemed wonderful until we arrived at Castell Brenin and found the doors locked.

'What are we going to do?' Kate cried in dismay. 'We can't stay out here all night!'

Even I was beginning to panic now. 'Keep your voice down!' I ordered. 'I'll think of something in a minute.

There must be some way to get back inside.'

'But what? The windows are all shut!'

We were huddled in a small group looking up at the rows of dark windows when there was a scraping sound of a casement window opening. In an instant, the boys disappeared; they scuttled across the quad as though they'd seen a vision out of hell. Then a face appeared and looked down at us without saying a word. It was Jan Webster in her dressing-gown.

I looked up, waiting for her to speak, but I waited in vain.

After about half a minute, which seemed more like half an hour, I said in a loud whisper, 'We're locked out, Jan.' I felt so stupid, stating the obvious.

'Are you?' Her voice was cold with sarcasm. 'You could have fooled me.'

There was more silence, and I felt sure that Kate was about to cry.

'What can we do?' I asked.

'That's a good question.' Jan Webster was obviously going to make us sweat; she wasn't going to let us in too soon.

'Who were those boys you were with?' she asked.

I knew that Kate was going to tell her, but I got in first.

'What boys? We've just been down to the lake . . . and forgot the time.'

She shook her head in disbelief, but then relented. 'I suppose I'd better let you in, hadn't I? Before Mr Keen hears you.'

A minute later, the door opened and Jan stood aside to let us in.

'I should report you for this, you understand that,

don't you? We're responsible for you. What if something had happened to you tonight?'

'We were all right,' I said lamely. 'We were with friends.'

'Oh, yes! Those two boys.'

'That's right.' I stopped. I could have kicked myself.

'Strange!' Jan said. 'I thought you said you were alone. Who were they anyway?'

I glanced a warning at Kate. 'Just two guys, that's all.'

'Huh!' Jan turned and walked up the stairs. 'I don't suppose one would be called Jeremy and the other Damien by any chance?'

They were waiting for us next morning as we walked down to the pool.

'What did she say last night?' Jeremy asked, falling in beside me.

'What do you think she said?'

'Did she ask who we were?' Damien seemed even more nervous than Jeremy.

'Of course not!' I gave him one of my sweetest smiles. 'She didn't have to, did she?'

I could swear that Jeremy went white. 'She knew?'

'Of course she knew.'

'But did she say anything?' There was desperation in his voice. 'Did she say what she was going to do?'

'She said she should report us.'

'Oh, no!' They were both white now.

I was going to let the two of them stew in their own juice for a little longer, but looking at them I just couldn't carry on.

'Oh, you two!' I said, relenting at last. 'Two fine

guys you turned out to be. At the first sign of trouble, you turned and ran.' Then I began to laugh, and surprisingly, Kate joined in. 'Of course she didn't report us. Just let us off with a warning, that's all.' Their faces changed as relief flooded their eyes.

'Thank goodness for that,' Jeremy said. 'Do you know, I don't think I slept a wink last night.'

Neither had I. But not for quite the same reason.

Chapter 7

It was a strange week. The first couple of days – a time when Jeremy and I got to know each other better and better – seemed to go slowly. We fell into the routine of lessons, lectures and rest periods, and spent most of our spare time with Kate and Damien. We often went jogging along country lanes; it was a chance to be alone together, to feel the gentle touch of his hand in mine.

But as soon as Tuesday came and went the time seemed to fly, and soon it was the last day. Long before that, I knew I had fallen in love with Jeremy, so as the final days sped by, I began to dread that last Friday together. Every time I thought of the Saturday morning when we would all depart and make our way across country, perhaps never to see each other again, there was a sinking feeling deep inside me. Tears would flood my eyes and I would have to turn away and force them back.

That's how it was that final Friday. I awoke as usual

to the sound of birds chirping away outside my window and with the sun slanting across my face. As soon as I opened my eyes I was aware that this was our last day at Castell Brenin and my heart plummeted to the pit of my stomach. I was being torn apart by conflicting emotions; half of me wanted to be with Jeremy, yet the other half wanted to stay in bed with my eyes shut, as though the very action would delay our inevitable separation.

Finally, I dragged myself out of bed and down to the pool-side to find Jeremy there before me, and one look into his eyes told me that he felt the same as I did.

He swam across the pool towards me and with one easy motion pulled himself on to the side.

'Hi!' he said, with a smile that was both sad and pleased. 'I came down early . . . I couldn't sleep.'

I sat next to him, my feet dangling in the water. I felt his damp shoulder against my warm skin and shivered.

'Me neither!' I said, wishing that I hadn't stayed in bed so long.

He gave a long drawn out sigh. 'Our last day, Alison. Tomorrow . . . ' He shrugged his shoulders with a helplessness that made me want to cry.

I shook my head, blinking away the tears. 'Let's forget tomorrow,' I said, my voice hoarse and strange. 'Let's enjoy today. Let's make the most of it . . . '

Suddenly, he jumped to his feet. 'You're right. We'll think of tomorrow when it comes. Race you to the end.'

He waited until I was on my feet, my toes at the edge of the pool. Then he grinned and nodded. Together, we launched ourselves into the water. I felt the coldness envelop me; I felt my whole body tingle with the shock, and then I was ploughing through the water.

Though I was a strong swimmer, Jeremy was even stronger and could have easily outstripped me. However, he stayed by my side and together we swam the whole length and with a mutual understanding, turned and swam back. Just swimming with him made me feel good. By the time we had returned, Mr Keen and all the other coaches were at the pool-side.

'Out, you two!' he commanded. 'You'll have plenty of time for informal swimming later.'

We joined Jan and the others and listened while she gave us our programme for the day. It was different from the other days, which I was glad of in a way because it gave me something else to think about, and since I loved swimming so much – almost as much as I loved Jeremy – I soon settled down to the routine exercises. From time to time, I'd catch Jeremy's eyes and we'd give each other our usual secret grin that meant so much.

Before long, the early morning training session was over and we were seated in the refectory eating breakfast. But my appetite had dwindled, so that all I could do was toy with my food.

Not so Jeremy. He glanced over and nodded at my plate of bacon, sausage and fried bread. 'Better eat up,' he said, helping himself to another slice of toast and layering it thickly with butter. 'You'll want all the energy you can get for the gala this afternoon.'

Though it was only a friendly competition, Jeremy was obviously taking it seriously. 'Don't want the other teams beating us,' he added with a grin that made me lose my appetite completely.

All the members of the course had been split into

four teams which they'd called Alpha, Beta, Gamma and Delta. Jeremy and I, together with Kate and Damien, had been placed in Delta. I mustn't let them down, I said to myself and taking Jeremy's advice, forced the food down.

Mr Keen announced his own rules regarding the gala. He informed us during the mid-morning break that two members only from each team would be allowed to compete in the finals of each event, and that each team would run its own heats to decide who they should be. And when we did that afternoon, we discovered how he'd arranged the teams in the first place. He'd obviously checked on our times over the week and made sure that the teams were well balanced.

I managed to get into the finals of the girls' one hundred metres freestyle, while both Jeremy and Damien were selected for the freestyle and backstroke events. Kate surprised herself, as well as us, by coming first in the breaststroke.

I also discovered something about myself. Though still, I was better at long distances, my speed had improved.

Shortly after three o'clock the gala proper began, and the excitement mounted as all eight competitors lined up for the start. Jeremy came first in the freestyle with Damien coming a close third. As for Kate and myself, we both succumbed to much stronger swimmers, coming fifth and sixth respectively in our events.

It soon became obvious that Gamma and Delta were the leaders, though there was very little in it, even at the end when the squadron was being swum. I was jumping up and down at the side of the pool as Jeremy, who had been chosen to represent Delta, came ploughing up the pool – and when he touched first, I could have jumped for joy. Come to think of it, I did.

Then came the waiting.

I knew it was going to be a near thing. Gamma had done so well that it was difficult to decide which of us had come first. We waited anxiously as the judges added up their totals; we watched them deliberate over their results and whisper urgently to each other. Then they nodded their heads, looked towards Mr Keen and held out a sheet of paper.

Mr Keen studied the results and then took up the microphone.

'We've all enjoyed ourselves this afternoon,' he began. 'And none more than me. My thanks to all of you . . . '

Come on! Come on! I thought. Please get the preliminaries over and done with. Oh, please!

'However, I'm sure you're all waiting for the result, so I'm going to announce the positions, in reverse order . . . '

A silence descended over the lido; only the gentle lapping of water could be heard.

'Fourth . . . ' he paused slightly, 'Beta.'

There was a groan of disappointment from Beta team who were huddled in a small group on the other side of the pool.

'Third . . . Alpha.'

There were groans again, interspersed with the occasional handclap.

Silence descended once more. Mr Keen glanced around at the spectators and teams aware that his next words would give the final order – the first as well as second.

'In second place . . .' he paused again. 'In second place . . . the team is . . . Gamma.'

There was an instant uproar. Delta had won. We had won. We all shouted with delight. Then we hugged each other, and then I became aware that I was hugging Jeremy and jumping up and down at the same time. When I became aware of who I was holding, I stopped jumping and looked up at him, feeling ridiculously shy.

He looked down with that so familiar grin. 'Hey! That was nice!' he said. 'Do it again!'

A last-night party had been organized in the common-room and after a special dinner, we made our way there. This time, Jeremy was waiting outside our dormitory block. He was wearing baggy jeans in faded blue denim and a brilliantly white tailored pilot shirt which hugged his muscular body and accentuated his tan and the tantalizing darkness of his hair. He completely took my breath away. Even Kate who had been forever warning me about getting too involved with a guy whom I'd probably never meet again was impressed. For once she understood how I felt about him – and why.

'You surprise me!' I exclaimed when the boys went to get some Coke from the small, make-shift bar in the corner of the room. 'I was beginning to suspect that you didn't like him.'

'Whatever gave you that idea?' she demanded hotly. 'I think he's a nice guy. I've always thought so . . . right from the very beginning. It's just . . . ' She shuffled uncomfortably on her seat. 'I don't want you to get hurt, that's all.'

'Oh, yes! And what about you and Damien? Don't tell me you don't feel anything for him!'

'Of course I do. I like him very much. But I've got the sense to realize that tomorrow it's going to be over – for good. And I remember that I've got a nice guy waiting for me at home, just as you have . . . '

For the first time that week, I thought about Phil, and almost kicked myself for feeling so guilty. What Phil and I had going for each other was all over now. It had been from the minute I first saw Jeremy, but before I could tell her so, he and Damien returned.

'Come on,' he said, taking my hand, 'let's dance. This is one of my favourites.'

I was in seventh heaven as we danced slowly across the floor until we got to the centre where no one could see us. Then he pulled me even closer and I clung to him desperately. We danced every dance together and later when the buffet had opened and we joined the crush for food, Jeremy suggested we went outside to eat.

Armed with disposable plates piled high with sandwiches, salads and sausage rolls, we sat on one of the benches in the quad and ate. Then after we had finished, we ambled down to the lake. There was a full moon that night; it shimmered on the still water and was so bright that it seemed almost like day.

Jeremy put his arm around me and drew me close.

'Oh, Alison!' he murmured softly in my ear. 'This has been a fantastic week . . . it really has.' I felt his lips gently kiss my hair. 'I don't know what I'm going to do without you.'

I looked up at him and felt my eyes mist over. 'Do you mean that? Do you really mean it?'

He smiled down at me and pulled me close. 'Of course I mean it, idiot! Don't you realize how much I love you?'

I didn't want that night to ever end, but all too soon we heard the shouts of people leaving the common-room and realized that the music had stopped and we had to return. Neither of us wanted Jan Webster losing her cool again. Having her report us to Mr Keen would have spoilt a perfect evening.

When he left me at the door, he took me in his arms and kissed me so sweetly, causing a surge of happiness to burst inside me.

That night I cried myself to sleep.

Chapter 8

For the first time that week I slept late. I don't know why. Perhaps it was the fact that the sun wasn't shining. Or that the song of the birds was muted. Or that I was completely worn out by all the crying I'd done the previous night. The reason wasn't important. Not seeing Jeremy off was, and I was furious with myself for not waking sooner.

I slung my legs out of bed, washed quickly and slipping on a pair of jeans and a T-shirt, hurried down to the refectory. Early breakfast was just finishing and as I arrived, Jeremy was coming out of the swing doors, accompanied by Damien.

His face lit up when he saw me. 'Hey! I thought we

were going to have breakfast together.'

'Oh, Jeremy. I know, but I slept late. Please forgive me.'

He took me by my arm and led me out of the building. 'Of course I forgive you, but not to worry. You're here now – that's all that matters.'

'I know! But I especially wanted to have breakfast with you. I wanted . . . oh, I don't know!'

Jeremy squeezed my arm. 'I wanted us to have the last few minutes together too, but like I said, you're here now, so forget it.'

I smiled fondly, while tears of sadness brimmed my eyes. 'Oh, Jeremy. I don't know what I'm going to do without you. Honestly, I don't.'

'I feel the same too,' he said glumly. 'But . . . ' He hesitated. 'Hey! I've just had an idea. Why don't you come and stay with us? You're not working or anything, are you? I mean, there's nothing to stop you?'

I shook my head, making a mental note to decline the job with Tesco's if they decided to employ me. Some things were more important than work.

'Are you sure your mother won't mind?'

He shook his head and snorted. 'Of course she won't. We've got bags of room. You can have the guest bedroom. It will be perfect.'

Guest room! If we had a guest room in our house, I thought, I'd be using it – to get away from that pest of a sister.

Jeremy was rummaging about in his pocket. He brought out a piece of paper and tore it in two.

'Here! We'd better exchange addresses. I don't know what's wrong with me. I almost forgot.' He scrawled the words on his piece. 'Don't forget your phone number,' he said. 'At least, we'll be able to talk to each other.'

Suddenly the world seemed brighter. At least there was some hope now. He took the scrap of paper with my address on it and thrust it into his hip pocket.

Then somebody called. It was Damien, loading the luggage on to their minibus.

'Better hurry up, Jeremy. I think the driver's getting impatient.'

He turned and gripped my hand. 'Looks like I have to be on my way.' We looked at each other helplessly and I thought for a moment he was going to kiss me – in front of everybody – but the possibility of being teased must have persuaded him otherwise. 'I'll phone you . . . soon,' he said huskily.

'Promise?' I said.

He nodded. 'Promise!'

He turned and walked quickly to the bus. I forced myself to smile as I heard the engine burst into life and saw the door shut behind him. Then it pulled away and as it turned the corner, the last I saw of Jeremy was him waving from the window.

Then a voice spoke at my side and I felt an arm circle my shoulder.

'I warned you, Alison Anderson,' Kate said gently. 'I warned you about getting hurt, didn't I?'

Mr Jarman called us in for breakfast. 'We'd better not be long,' he said before joining the other coaches on the rostrum. 'The sooner we leave, the sooner we'll be home.'

I didn't care. Though I wanted to see Mum and Dad and Paul and even my pest of a sister Julie, part of me had gone with Jeremy and I knew I wouldn't be the same again until we met.

Kate didn't say much on the first part of the journey home; she had the sense to leave me alone with my thoughts as I gazed blindly out of the window of the bus seeing nothing but Jeremy's face. As I did so, a great void grew inside me. He was travelling south while I was travelling north, and every minute that passed took us further and further away from each other. Not even the promise of a holiday at his place could brighten my spirits and in the end, Kate put her hand on my arm.

'Come on, Alison,' she said gently and sympathetically. 'Things aren't as bad as they seem.'

Weren't they? I shrugged her hand away. They were worse.

'I mean, Phil will be waiting for you when you get home. We can all go to the disco tonight – you, me, Phil and Kenny . . . '

I turned abruptly. 'I can't.'

'Don't be ridiculous! We always go to the Saturday night disco.'

'I know. I didn't mean that.'

She frowned. 'Don't tell me you're too tired.'

I lost my temper. 'Of course I'm not tired.'

'Well, then?' Kate was peeved at the sharpness in my voice.

'Oh, Kate. Surely you must understand! I can't go. Because . . . because I can't see Phil again . . . ever.'

'Can't see Phil again? But why not?'

'Oh, Kate. Do I have to spell it out?' I breathed in deeply to curb my temper. 'I'm going to finish with him, that's why.'

She looked at me in amazement. 'Because of Jeremy.'

'Yes! Because of Jeremy!'

She stared at me for a moment without saying a word; then she shook her head. 'But Alison! Jeremy is just someone you met on a course – almost like a holiday romance. It was great while it lasted. But now it's all over.'

I gritted my teeth. 'It's not all over. He's asked me to come down and stay with him.'

'When?'

'He didn't say . . . anytime . . . '

She sat back in her seat. 'Huh! I'll believe that when it happens.'

If we were ever close to having our first real quarrel, it was then. But wisely Kate didn't pursue the matter and I was so angry that I couldn't say a word. All I could do was glare out of the window and fume.

Then about five minutes later, she sighed. 'Oh, Alison! I know you think I don't understand, but I do, really I do.'

'How can you?' I asked bitterly. 'You didn't like Damien all that much.'

She went quiet and when I glanced at her, I could see she was hurt. 'That's where you're wrong. I liked Damien very much. Why do you think I didn't come down till the last moment this morning?'

I turned and looked at her. 'Because you didn't want to see him?'

She shook her head. 'Because I didn't think it was wise to see him. There's a difference. I told him last night I wouldn't. I told him about Kenny and he said he understood.' She paused and for a moment I had a strong feeling that she was going to tell me something about Jeremy. Then she went on. 'So you see, sometimes it's better to make a complete break. It's often easier that way.'

I was silent for a long time after that. I kept thinking that Kate seemed far more grown up in her attitude than I'd given her credit for. Yet I kept thinking too that if she had fallen as deeply in love with Damien as I had with Jeremy, then she shouldn't be quite as objective as she was. Thoughts kept spinning around in my mind, and though I became more and more confused, one thing was clear. I had to finish with Phil. Of that I was sure. And I told Kate so when the coach stopped for lunch.

She wasn't impressed. 'That's up to you. But if you ask me, you're making the biggest mistake of your whole life. Phil's a nice guy and you don't appreciate him. And if you ask me, you'll never know what you've lost until it's too late.'

But I wasn't asking her. I had made up my mind, and that was an end to it.

It was barely an hour after lunch when we arrived home. I saw the road sign which said 'Grimborough 5 miles', and about fifteen minutes later we were driving through the suburbs. I could actually smell the pollution; there was the heavy smell of oil and diesel fumes in the air which made me feel physically sick.

Why, oh why, couldn't we live somewhere nicer? I sighed. Somewhere like Beckhaven. Better still, Beckhaven itself.

There was a huge empty hole in the pit of my stomach, and not even the sight of my mother waiting outside the lido could dispel it.

Her face was beaming as she came towards me.

'Darling!' she said, giving me a hug that crushed the breath out of me. 'Did you have a nice time?'

I gave her the merest hint of a smile. 'Yes – it was great.'

She looked at me closely. 'You don't sound as though you did. Are you sure?'

She was beginning to irritate me. I didn't want to speak. I wanted to get home and fling myself on my bed and think of Jeremy.

'Oh, Mum!' I sighed, curbing with difficulty the sharp words that were on my lips. 'Of course I'm sure. It's just . . . I'm just tired, that's all.'

She picked up my case and carried it to the car.

'Well, if you're sure that's all.'

'I'm sure,' I replied laconically, trying to avoid her examining eyes. 'Please! I just want to get home.'

She didn't say anything until she dropped Kate off at her house, and I was glad. I stared out at the grimy, dingy streets and thought of the place where Jeremy lived. He had described it so often, I felt I knew it. The air was so clean and fresh there and I longed to be there with him. Instead, through no fault of my own – through no fault of anyone's – I lived in a Midlands town that I hated. I'd do anything to get away.

But before we arrived home, Mum pulled into a lay-by outside a supermarket.

'Now then, my girl!' she said in that determined way I knew so well. 'You said back there that everything was all right. But it isn't . . . I just know it isn't. So I think you'd better tell me what's happened. You met somebody there, didn't you?'

I nodded miserably. Yet at the same time, I was glad she knew.

'I see. What's his name?'

'Jeremy,' I muttered hoarsely. 'And oh, Mum! He's the most fantastic boy I've ever known.'

Her frown deepened. 'You and this Jeremy – did anything happen?'

My frown matched hers. 'Happen?'

'Yes! Happen!' She gave a snort of exasperation. 'Oh, come on, Alison. You're old enough. You know what I mean . . . '

Then the penny dropped and I felt my face go red. 'Oh, Mum! Of course nothing like that happened. What sort of girl do you think I am?'

She took a deep breath and breathed out slowly. 'I know the kind of girl you are, Alison. But I don't know what this Jeremy's like, do I?'

I shook my head. 'He's not like that. He'd never do anything to hurt me . . . I know he wouldn't.'

But I could tell she wasn't convinced. She switched on the ignition and looking over her right shoulder, pulled away, slotting neatly into the Saturday afternoon traffic.

'And what about Phil?' she asked, glancing at me. 'You know how he feels about you.'

I shook my head. 'I can't help it, Mum. I'm going to have to tell him. I'm going to have to break it off . . . '

'When?'

'Right now. As soon as I get home.'

But Mum was in one of her determined moods.

'Oh, no you don't, my girl. Not tonight you don't.'

I looked at her in dismay. What had she let me in for now?

Chapter 9

'Why? Why not tonight?' I demanded.

My mother glanced anxiously, her eyes wary. 'Well, I don't suppose you remember, but it's our wedding anniversary today . . . '

Shame chased suspicion from my mind. 'Oh, Mum! I forgot – and I haven't bought you a present.'

She smiled fondly, glancing in the mirror and pulling into the outer lane.

'That doesn't matter, darling. I didn't expect one . . . ' She paused and I knew it wasn't just that she was concentrating on the traffic. 'Anyway, your father thought it might be a good idea if we went out for dinner tonight.'

'We?' I asked as suspicion returned.

'Not the children . . . I've got a baby sitter for them. Just you . . . ' She hesitated again. ' . . . and Phil, of course . . . '

I sank into my seat and folded my arms. 'No, Mum! I'm not going with Phil. I've just told you; it's all over between us.'

Again there was that silence. 'I know, but you see, I've already invited him.'

I sat up. 'Oh, no! You haven't, have you?'

'I'm sorry, darling. But I wasn't to know that . . . that you were going to feel as you do when you returned. After all, when you went away, everything seemed all right between you.'

'Well, you'll just have to un-invite him, won't you?'

By this time we had reached home. She pulled into the drive and switched off the engine.

She shook her head. 'But we can't do that, Alison. It would be much too embarrassing.'

I glared at her. 'What about me? Don't you think it's going to be embarrassing for me – going out with Phil after I've told him it's all over between us?'

She made no attempt to get out of the car. She sat there for a few moments and then gave a deep sigh.

'I realize that. But honestly, I can't see what we're going to do unless . . . '

'Unless what?'

'Unless you told him tomorrow instead.'

Tears were pricking my eyes. I shook my head. 'I can't, Mum. I can't go out with him tonight. Please don't ask me to.'

I opened the door, stumbled out of the car, and rushed into the house, passing Julie on the way upstairs. I slammed my bedroom door behind me and flung myself on to my bed.

Why must parents be so difficult? I kept asking myself over and over again; why must they try and organize your life for you?

The door opened and Julie entered. She bounced on to my bed.

'Who's this new boyfriend?'

'Mind your own business! Anyway, how do you know about him?'

My scowl didn't deter her. 'I heard Mum telling Dad about him – said his name was Jeremy . . . said you were going to break it off with Phil . . . ' She hesitated and when I made no reply, went on.

'If you ask me, you're being stupid,' she said airily.

'Nobody's asking you!'

'I like Phil. I wouldn't give him up for a stupid guy I met on holiday.'

I sat up, leaning on one elbow, and gave her a blistering smile. It seemed that everyone was on Phil's side – even my kid sister.

'You're too young to have a boyfriend,' I muttered.

She stood up and laughed. 'Too young? I've had loads of boyfriends.' She looked down haughtily. 'I'm thirteen, remember. I'm not a kid any more.'

I was beginning to get exasperated with her – with everybody – and would have laughed had I not been so desperately unhappy.

'Then go out and find another one to add to your list,' I snapped bitterly. 'Just leave me in peace.'

'Very well . . . ' She shrugged her shoulders and turned. 'Be like that. I know when I'm not wanted.'

After she'd left, I lay back on my pillow and gave a deep sigh. Everybody seemed to like Phil: Kate, Mum, Dad, Julie and, I had to admit, even I liked him.

But I liked Jeremy better. Why couldn't people understand that?

There was a knock on the door.

'Who is it now?' I asked in a resigned voice. I obviously wasn't to be allowed any peace.

The door opened and Dad's face appeared. 'It's me,' he said with an awkward grin. 'All right if I come in?'

Then without waiting for a reply, he entered and closed the door behind him.

'Hey! What's all this commotion about? How come you never came to see me when you arrived?

I swung my legs off the bed. 'Sorry, Dad. I was . . . ' I gave a helpless shrug. 'Oh, I don't know!'

He grinned, sat down beside me and put his arm around my shoulder.

'I hear you've met another guy. Must be quite something – not like you to fly into a temper so readily.'

I smiled weakly. 'He is. That's why I can't go out with Phil again.'

'I see!' He frowned and bit his lip. 'I think I can understand that.'

'You're the only one who does then!'

He pulled me closer. 'No, I'm not. Your mother understands too. It's just . . . it creates an awkward situation, that's all.'

'That's not my fault, Dad.'

'No!' he conceded. 'But that doesn't help your mother. She asked Phil out tonight because she naturally assumed that you'd want her to. I mean, if you hadn't met . . . what's his name?'

'Jeremy.'

'If you hadn't met Jeremy, and we hadn't asked Phil to come out with us tonight, you'd have been furious, wouldn't you?'

I nodded cautiously, not knowing exactly where this conversation was leading.

'You'd have said we were insulting him, wouldn't you?'

I nodded again.

'Well . . . ' He took a deep breath. 'If we told him now he couldn't come after all, that would be just as insulting. Surely you must see that.'

'But Dad. What can I do? I can't go out with him again!'

'You won't be going out with him, will you? He'll be coming out with us – all of us. You won't be alone with him. It would just be like going out with a crowd.'

I could see now where his logic was leading.

'All I'm asking you to do is delay telling him. I know it may sound unfair – both to Phil and you – but I'm only asking you to do it for your mother's sake. She really has been looking forward to tonight. And you'll notice that she wanted you to be with us.' He ruffled my hair. 'Come on, love. What do you say? Do it for your mother. She'd do anything for you.'

He made me realize that to refuse would have been churlish, so I just sighed and nodded glumly.

'But I'm going to have to tell him soon,' I said with determination.

Dad nodded sombrely. 'Of course. You must do what you think is right. After all, you're a big girl now, Alison.'

There was a huge bunch of flowers in the living room when I went down, and the look on Mum's face now that Dad had told her of my decision, made me feel glad. But even so, I felt sick at the thought of meeting Phil that evening and trying to act normally.

He arrived just before seven, his face beaming with delight at seeing me, but when he tried to kiss me on my lips and I turned my head away, I noticed the frown that furrowed his forehead.

'Enjoy the course?' he asked as I led him quickly into the living room. The less time I spent alone with him the better. For both our sakes.

'Yeah! All right!' I replied without enthusiasm.

He gave a polite non-committal smile. 'Doesn't sound as though you did.'

'A course is a course. It's no big deal.'

Mum was still upstairs getting ready, but Dad was sitting in the armchair, reading the football results in the evening paper. He looked up and took off his reading spectacles.

'Hello, Phil!' He was being more affable than usual, and I sensed that Phil suspected something was wrong. 'Well, make yourself at home.'

Phil sat down opposite him while Dad went to the foot of the stairs and called up to Mum.

'You'd better hurry up,' he yelled. 'I've reserved a table for half past seven . . . '

Then he returned to the living room. 'I see Albion are doing well,' he said, with just a little too much enthusiasm, as though he was trying to compensate for my lack of it. 'They won again today . . . '

Phil said nothing. He just gave a smile.

It was a disaster of an evening. I was moody and silent for most of the time, and it took a very real effort on my part to talk to Phil. Dad drove us to a large hotel about five miles south of Grimborough. It was an imposing building, set at the end of a long drive and with a large car park at the front and rear. As we drove up to it, floodlighting illuminated the front, giving it an air of grandeur. It was the same inside: thick pile carpets you sank into and crisp white tablecloths with rows of cutlery.

Not until Mum squeezed my hand under the table and gave me an encouraging smile, did I make the effort to be friendly. But it was hard forcing Jeremy out of my mind – trying against my will to blot him out. Dad was chatting away heartily, making jokes and trying to keep the party merry, and it seemed such a shame that he had to do that just because of me.

So I perked up and pretended that everything was all right, but it took a lot more than that to fool Phil. He knew now – felt it instinctively – that something was wrong, and when we left I could tell that he was waiting for us to be alone together. Dad drove us home just after eleven o'clock and as he pulled up outside the house, I prayed that Mum wouldn't ask Phil in for coffee. I wanted to get to bed – to be on my own and close my eyes and dream of Jeremy.

But as we all got out of the car, she turned to him.

'Would you like to come in for coffee?' adding unnecessarily, 'We always have one before we go to bed.'

Phil jumped at the offer. 'Yes – I'd like that, Mrs Anderson.'

I deliberately helped Mum with the coffee, just so that I wouldn't be left alone with him.

'Why did you do that?' I whispered urgently.

'Do what?' Mum looked at me with feigned innocence.

'You know what. Ask him in for coffee, that's what. You know I'm tired.'

She spooned the coffee into the mugs and looked at me with knowing disbelief. 'It's only half past eleven, Alison. What's happened to the girl who likes to stay out until two in the morning?'

'I told you. I'm tired.'

She poured hot milk into the mugs and placed them on a tray. Then she handed the tray to me.

'You won't have to stay up long. Just long enough to drink your coffee.'

I carried the tray into the living room and placed it on the low table in front of the settee where Phil and

Dad were sitting. I gave Phil a flicker of a smile as I handed him his mug.

'Thanks,' he said, one of the few words he'd uttered since coming in. But his eyes were watching me as he drank, silently questioning me and the darkness of his frown deepened.

Then he finished his drink and stood up. 'I think I'd better go, it's getting late . . . '

With growing reluctance, I went to the front door with him, deliberately closing the door that led into the hall so that Mum and Dad couldn't hear what I had decided to say to him.

But it was Phil who took the initiative. 'What's wrong, Alison?' he asked as he opened the door. 'What have I done?'

I had been about to tell him what I'd rehearsed all that evening as we sat around the table at the hotel, but his question took me by surprise. It threw me into confusion and I forgot the words.

'Nothing!'

He spun round. 'Come off it. I know something's wrong. I can feel it. I've felt it all evening. Is it something I've said?'

I felt my face go hot. 'Of course not.'

'Then what is it?'

I hesitated for a moment as I tried to pluck up courage to tell him, but I hesitated too long.

'Oh, what's the use!' he said angrily. 'It doesn't matter what I do, nothing seems to satisfy you.'

And turning, he stormed down the drive and vanished into the darkness of the night.

Chapter 10

The following week disaster struck. When I checked the drawer of my bedside cabinet for the scrap of paper on which Jeremy's phone number was written, I couldn't find it. I remembered clearly placing it where I imagined it would be safe, but though I turned out the jumble of tights, socks and pants, there was no sign of it. I even accused Julie of having raided my drawer to borrow something, but she strenuously denied it.

Eventually, I had to accept that it was lost and almost screamed with anger and frustration. Now there was no way I could contact him.

I spent days pining for him, hoping that each time the phone rang it would be him and trying to keep away from Phil. All I wanted to do was lie alone in my bedroom, listening to smoochy records. Phil called by one evening, but Mum told him I wasn't well and that I was asleep in bed. I could hear her telling him at the front door, and it made me feel so guilty to have persuaded her to lie like that. It didn't make my mother feel good either.

She came up to me immediately after. 'Honestly, Alison, I don't know why I let you persuade me to lie for you. If you only knew how I felt, you wouldn't have asked me. But I'll tell you one thing – next time, you can tell him yourself.'

I lifted myself up and leaned on one elbow. 'Oh,

Mum! You can't do that.'

'Can't I? Just you wait and see.'

'But, Mum!' I protested as tears stung my eyes. 'I can't see Phil. You know how I feel . . . '

'Then you must tell him the truth,' she said firmly. 'It's not fair to treat him like this, to keep him dangling just in case this Jeremy doesn't phone.'

I felt my face flush. I too had wondered if that were the real reason behind my reluctance to tell Phil; after all, I'd had the chance and squandered it. And I knew then, as I turned my head away, that it was true. I was making use of him – just in case things didn't work out between me and Jeremy.

Mum sat down on my bed and held my hand. 'Oh, Alison! I honestly don't know what to make of you. It isn't like you to behave like this. Surely you must realize that holiday romances don't work.'

I shook my head. Jeremy had said he loved me; he had said he would phone. He would. I knew he would.

'It wasn't a holiday romance. I've told you – he meant it when he said he'd phone.'

'I'm sure he did . . . at the time. But now he's back at home . . . '

'He's forgotten all about me? Is that what you mean?'

Mum looked down. 'Well, it is a possibility.'

I shook my head firmly. 'No! You don't know him, Mum. He wouldn't do a thing like that.'

'Perhaps he wouldn't . . . '

'No perhaps! You don't know him.'

'Neither do you, love. I mean, you've only known him for a few days . . . '

'It was a whole week.'

'All right. A whole week. But that's not long enough to get to know anyone really well.'

I turned over with my back to her and buried my head in my pillow. I didn't want to listen to her say such things about Jeremy. They weren't true. They couldn't be. She sat silently at my side for a moment or two and then squeezed my shoulder.

'Why don't you come downstairs?' she suggested as she rose to her feet. 'I don't like you lying up here all the time. On your own.'

I heard her go out, closing the door softly behind her, and for about half an hour I lay there thinking of Jeremy. Perhaps he had lost that scrap of paper he'd thrust so carelessly into his hip pocket. Perhaps that's why he hadn't phoned.

Then I had an idea. Though I couldn't find his number through directory enquiries – I couldn't remember his address – perhaps the local library might be able to help. Perhaps they kept telephone directories there for the whole country. It was worth a try, and if they did, I should then be able to find it. After all, Sinclair wasn't that common a name.

The next morning, I was out of bed and dressed before nine o'clock – much to my mother's surprise – and made my way into town. I had to wait around for almost half an hour because the library didn't open to the public until half past nine, but as soon as I saw the young assistant open the glass-fronted doors, I charged up the stairs to the reference library on the first floor. The librarian looked up in surprise as I walked in.

'My first customer,' he exclaimed with a smile, glancing over his thick horn-rimmed spectacles. 'And what can I do for you, miss?'

I explained what I was looking for.

'No problem,' he said and led me to an alcove in the far corner where the directories were kept.

'You should find the Beckhaven numbers in here,' he said, taking a large book down from the shelf. 'I imagine you know how to find the person you want.'

He left me alone to scan through the pages. I soon discovered that Sinclair was a much more common name in Beckhaven than I thought, not that it presented me with any real problem. Jeremy's mother was a doctor and there was only one doctor with the surname Sinclair, a Doctor Daphne Sinclair with two numbers – one for her surgery and one for her residence.

My heart soared. Now I would be able to phone him.

I was so happy that even meeting Phil as he cycled through the town centre couldn't dampen my delight.

'Feeling better?' He made no mention of having stormed off that Saturday night.

I shocked myself at the ease with which I lied to him.

'Yes. I had this terrible cold – that's why I stayed in bed . . . '

As we sauntered along, Phil was talking about something, though I hardly heard what he said because I was thinking what I'd say to Jeremy when I phoned him that evening.

'You haven't answered me . . . ' Phil's voice brought me out of my dreams.

'Sorry. I was thinking. What did you say?'

'I asked you if you'd like to come to a gig at the Coachhouse,' he repeated. 'Double Trouble will be there.'

Normally I would have jumped at the chance to see one of my favourite local groups, but this time I wasn't particularly interested.

'Oh!' I said vaguely. 'When is it?'

He shook his head. 'You haven't heard a thing I've said, have you? It's in two weeks – two weeks this Saturday to be exact.'

'I see.' I thought quickly. I didn't really want to go, but perhaps Mum was right. I shouldn't cut myself off from all my friends because of Jeremy. Besides my happiness made me feel generous. 'Will Kate and Kenny be going?'

'Of course. I told you – Kenny is getting the tickets.'

No harm in going in a foursome, I thought. I nodded. 'Yes . . . all right.'

But I could see Phil wasn't too happy at my attitude; my tone had shown him that I didn't care one way or the other. He frowned and shook his head.

'All right. I'll tell Kenny tonight to get them.' He glanced at me cautiously as though wondering whether or not to ask his next question. 'You going to the swimming club tonight?'

I'd forgotten it was Friday. Up till then I'd not been that keen on going, but now that I could phone Jeremy, the world seemed so different. I felt my enthusiasm returning.

'Yes! Why not!'

'Then I'll see you afterwards?'

I nodded. 'If you like.'

'See you tonight, then.'

As I watched him go, I felt so sorry. I knew what he was going through, but there was nothing I could do about it.

I had intended phoning Jeremy soon after six o'clock,

but as the time approached, some of my euphoria evaporated. The doubts that my mother had sown in my mind came to the fore. What if he hadn't lost my phone number, I asked myself? What if he had decided not to get in touch with me? If that were the case, what would he say when he heard my voice?

I could just imagine the embarrassed silence followed by a gushing explanation of why he hadn't phoned. I actually had the receiver in my hand, my index finger had dialled the first three numbers, when the doubts came crowding in, making my stomach sink as though a heavy weight had been thrown into it.

I placed the receiver back on its rest, as courage deserted me for the second time that week – first with Phil and now with Jeremy.

Kate called round just before seven and together we ambled along to the sports centre. As I walked to the pool side, tucking my hair into my cap, I smelt the tang of chlorine, and it brought back the previous week so vividly that I almost cried. It had been a week, a whole week, since that last night at Castell Brenin when Jeremy and I had wandered down to the lake. I remembered the way he'd held my hand; I remembered his loving words; I remembered the way he'd kissed me and set my whole body tingling in a way I'd never experienced before.

It seemed like a lifetime away.

I stood at the pool-side and launched myself into the air. I felt the cool water close over me, felt the familiar exhilaration thrill me, and then I was ploughing along, my fingers churning up the water. I recalled Jeremy swimming along at my side, and the feeling was so strong that for a moment, when Kate joined me, I thought it was him.

I was glad now that I had come – that I hadn't given in to my despondency. Somehow just being in the water made me feel nearer to Jeremy.

Kate and I swam two lengths, arriving back as Mr Jarman came in.

We padded to where he was standing, surrounded by the others, and it was just like the time three weeks previously. I could have sworn I was reliving the experience.

He held an envelope in his hands, and as he took out the letter, he grinned at me.

'Thought you all might like to know we've had an invitation . . . ' He paused. 'No, not to return to Castell Brenin – that will come next year.' He paused again as he unfolded the sheet of headed notepaper. 'This comes from Beckhaven Swimming Club.'

I caught my breath. From Beckhaven. I could feel my heart pounding as tears of joy blurred my eyes. But why? My mind spun with possibilities.

'They've invited us to take part in their annual sea swim next Saturday.' As he explained all about it, my mind was in a dream world where all my wishes were coming true. 'It's a good chance to gain experience . . . especially you, Alison. Well? What do you say?'

I didn't give anyone else a chance. 'Yes, please!' I cried. 'That will be fantastic.'

Everybody laughed, and I blushed.

Mr Jarman grinned at me. 'Oh, yes! I almost forgot. I have a special message for you, Alison. It seems there's a young man at Beckhaven . . . ' He pretended to read the letter. ' . . . calls himself Jeremy Sinclair or something. Says he's going to phone you tonight between nine and ten.'

I thought at that moment I might burst with joy. He glanced around at us all. 'I take it you're all in agreement, like Alison here . . . ' There was a murmur from the others and he nodded. 'Great. I'll make the necessary arrangements then.' He clapped his hands. 'Right. Let's get down to practise. We'll go for distance tonight.'

I spent the whole of the two hours in a dream, going through all the motions automatically. All I could think of was that Jeremy hadn't forgotten me and that in just over a week I'd be seeing him again.

I didn't meet Phil that evening. I left early, rushed out of the changing rooms and ran almost all the way home.

Chapter 11

My mother was on the phone as I hurried up the path. I could see her distorted figure against the heavily patterned glass of the front door. I gave a cry of exasperation and let myself in. When my mother was talking to someone, she could be hours, and if Jeremy should try to phone and find the number engaged, he might give up – and where would I be then? But I was about to be surprised. She looked up, smiled, and said, 'Hold on. She's just arrived.' She held the receiver out to me. 'It's for you . . . Jeremy . . . '

I couldn't believe it. I snatched the phone from her.

'Jeremy! It's me. Alison.' My heart was pounding madly as I cried with relief. 'I've just come back from the swimming club. Mr Jarman told us about the sea swim.'

'Are you coming?' I hardly listened to his words; I just listened to his voice.

'Of course I'm coming . . . ' Tears of joy were streaming ridiculously down my face and I sniffed them back.

'And did he tell you that my mother had invited you to stay with us?'

'No . . . no, he didn't.'

'Well, she has.'

Although happiness bubbled up inside me, I felt a twinge of anxiety at the thought of meeting his mother for the first time and staying the night at his place.

What would she think of me?

'Will that be all right?'

'Of course it will be all right,' I replied.

'Great! I'll be able to show you around. There are some fantastic places around here, and we'll go to the disco on Saturday night – you'll like it.'

I had no doubts in my mind about that and we went on talking for about ten minutes until Jeremy said he'd better ring off.

'Someone might be trying to get in touch with my mother,' he explained. 'She might be called out . . . '

'That's all right. I understand.'

We wished each other goodnight and Jeremy added, 'See you in a week! I can't tell you how much I'm looking forward to it!'

I put down the phone and literally floated into the

living room. I hadn't asked him why he hadn't phoned earlier. It wasn't important. Not any more.

Dad looked up from the television and grinned. 'This is the first time I've seen you smile this week. This Jeremy has a remarkable influence over you.'

But not even the 'this Jeremy' remark could offend me now. I just smiled more than ever.

'Well!' my mother remarked. 'Aren't you going to tell us what he said?'

'He didn't say anything.'

'Then he took a long time saying it.'

'Oh, Mum! You know what I mean!' I hesitated for a moment. 'But he did ask me to come and stay with him.'

My mother arched her eyebrows. 'Oh, did he now! I'm not sure I approve of that.'

'Oh, Mum!' A pang of anxiety stabbed at my heart. Surely she wasn't going to prevent my going. Not now. 'Why not?'

'Because I don't know him. That's why not.'

'But, Mum! I'm not a kid any more. I'm sixteen . . . '

'That's why I'm worried . . . '

Dad looked at her and frowned. 'You said he sounded like a nice young man.'

My heart gave a leap. Trust Dad to come to my help.

'Perhaps I did. But we don't really know him, do we? Anyone can sound nice on the phone.'

'Now you're being irrational. She's not going to stay in the house alone with him.'

'No,' she began slowly and then stopped as a look of alarm flashed in her eyes. 'At least, I hope not . . . '

'So why are you worrying? Surely we can trust our daughter to be sensible.'

They were discussing me as though I wasn't even in the room, and Julie who had long abandoned her interest in the television programme was listening with almost bated breath.

'She might do something stupid,' she said.

Dad turned on her sternly. 'Who asked you to comment? You shouldn't have been listening.'

'And you shouldn't be talking about me as though I wasn't even in the room!' I complained. 'You haven't asked me why he's invited me to stay yet.'

Mum glanced at me. 'Oh! And is there some special reason?'

'Of course there is,' I cried in exasperation. 'The club's been invited to take part in a long-distance swim across Beckhaven Bay. It's a yearly event which takes place every August. That's why I'm going,' I said innocently. 'What other reason could there be?'

My mother arched her eyebrows again in sceptical disbelief. 'Now you're making me more suspicious than ever,' she said pointedly.

But I knew that really the arguments were all over. They both knew how keen I was on long-distance swimming, and though they might have had reservations about Jeremy, they wouldn't have prevented me taking part in the race. I told them all that Mr Jarman had told us that evening and soon my staying at Jeremy's house was approved.

'And what about Phil?' my mother asked when we were alone in the kitchen preparing our late-night drink. 'Does he know yet about Jeremy, or that you're going to see him next week?'

I shook my head. 'I haven't seen him,' I said, conveniently omitting that even if I had I probably wouldn't have told him everything. 'So he can't know, can he? Unless Kate tells him.'

My mother frowned. 'Well, you know by now I don't approve of the way you're treating him. You should be honest with him. At least, he'd be able to make some decision then, even if you can't. Try putting yourself in his shoes. How would you feel if he treated you this way?'

But she was taking the whole thing too seriously, I said to myself as I carried the tray into the living room. After all, it wasn't as if we were engaged or anything like that. We were just good friends and I could do just as I liked. But even as I said it, I knew it wasn't true, and I shut the guilt firmly out of my mind.

Phil called round the next morning. It was a beautiful day and since I couldn't be sure that Julie might not blurt out something about Jeremy's phone call the previous night, I suggested a walk around the park. Besides, I honestly didn't want him to be hurt, and I knew that he would be if he knew about Jeremy.

Why, oh, why did life have to be so difficult when you grew up? I asked myself.

We ambled along the wide paths, past large flower-beds until we came to the tennis courts at the far end. We sat on one of the wooden benches and watched a couple as they played.

'Did you meet anybody on that course last week?' Phil asked suddenly, pretending to be watching the game.

'I met lots of people. After all, there were lots of people there.'

'Yeah, I know that, but . . . ' He paused awkwardly.

'I meant someone special . . . '

I felt myself go hot and prayed that I wasn't blushing.

'Of course not!' As an afterthought I added, 'I did meet a guy from Beckhaven. We had the same coach.'

'I see . . . This place – Beckhaven – is that where you're going next weekend?'

I glanced at him sharply. 'How did you know about that?'

He shrugged his shoulders. 'Kate mentioned it last night. As a matter of fact, she didn't stop talking about it, even though she probably won't take part.'

So Kate had talked freely, as I'd suspected she would.

'That's right,' I replied, seeing the futility of lying. 'She's coming as one of the supporters. And as you know, we've been invited to take part in their annual swim.'

'And you'll be staying at this guy's house? The one who had the same coach as you?'

I began to wonder what else Kate had told him.

'That's right. It seems we're all staying with Beckhaven Club members. I think Kate's staying at Damien's house . . . she met him at Castell Brenin.'

Phil nodded, still watching the game though I could tell he wasn't concentrating on it. 'I know. She told us last night . . . '

'So why are you asking me now?' I demanded.

'No reason. Just couldn't understand why you hadn't told me yourself, that's all.'

'Look, Phil. I don't know why you're behaving like this. Surely the explanation's simple . . . '

'Is it?'

'Of course it is. Let's be fair! You haven't given me a chance to tell you.'

He frowned. 'No. Perhaps you're right. I haven't, have I?'

'No, you haven't!' I replied, just a little angry.

'And you would have told me in time?'

'Of course I would have. I would have told you this morning if you'd given me the chance.' I stood up and began to walk away. 'Honestly, Phil. You'd swear I had something to hide.'

He caught up with me before I had gone more than a dozen yards. He grabbed my arm and pulled me to face him.

'Sorry, Alison. I just had to know. You must realize just how much I like you.' He let go of my arm and we walked together back to the house. 'About tonight,' he said as we arrived at the garden gate. 'Are you still coming to the disco?'

I nodded. 'Of course I'm coming.'

He smiled, though I couldn't help noticing the sadness in his eyes. 'Great!' he said. 'Pick you up? The usual time? And by the way – about that gig – I've got those tickets.'

I watched him walk away and wave as he turned the corner. Mum was right. Phil was a nice guy and I cared for him, but I loved Jeremy. So what could I possibly do?

Surprisingly, I enjoyed myself at the disco that night, far more than I expected, though as we danced, I couldn't help wondering what Jeremy was doing at that moment. Probably doing just what I was doing, I convinced myself – dancing at a disco and (hopefully) thinking of me and longing for the coming week to fly.

Phil seemed a lot happier too. The four of us walked home along darkened streets, laughing and giggling, and for an hour or so the pangs of longing I felt for Jeremy lifted, and briefly I was able to enjoy myself.

I even let Phil kiss me, but as I got into bed, Julie had to spoil it all.

'I saw you,' she said accusingly. 'I saw you kiss Phil. What would your precious Jeremy say if he knew?' she added with a note of sarcasm in her voice.

'What's it to do with you?' I snapped. 'Haven't you anything better to do than spy on me?'

But as I lay in the darkness, I couldn't help feeling sorry again for Phil. Perhaps I was two-timing him. But then, I said to myself, turning on my side and hugging my pillow, all's fair in love and war.

They were words I was to remember; words I'd grow to regret.

Chapter 12

Phil grew moodier and moodier all that week as Saturday approached. It was just like the week before we went to Castell Brenin. Then on the Friday evening we met Mr Jarman to finalize the arrangements.

'We'll leave as near to nine o'clock tomorrow morning as possible. It's a far longer journey than the Castell Brenin one so I suggest we meet outside at nine o'clock sharp, load our cases and get away by nine-fifteen at the latest.'

'What time do you think we'll get there?' I asked, trying to sound as casual as I could, though inside I was tingling with excitement. I was longing to see Jeremy again.

'Hard to say,' he replied. 'It depends on the traffic. We'll make our way down the M5 to Bristol, get on the M4 and then cut south through Salisbury.'

'We'll be stopping for lunch, I hope,' said Steve Lawson.

Mr Jarman nodded. 'We'll have something at the Leigh Delamere Services on the M4. Bring some sandwiches if you like.'

'But when will we get there?' I asked again.

'About four o'clock,' he replied, adding with a laugh, 'as long as the minibus doesn't break down.'

I crossed my fingers behind my back. If that happens, I think I'll just die, I said silently to myself. But now at least I had something definite to tell Jeremy when I phoned him that night.

Phil was waiting as Kate and I left the small room where we'd met for the final briefing. He must, I realized, have been waiting there for some time, and when he smiled at me, there was apprehension in his eyes.

'Hi!' I said in surprise. 'I thought you and Kenny were playing squash tonight.'

He gave an awkward shrug. 'I didn't fancy it. Thought I'd come over and see what you two are doing.'

'Well,' I began, 'I should be getting home and having an early night. We're leaving early tomorrow morning.'

'Not that early,' protested Kate. 'You can't call nine

o'clock early.' She turned to Phil. 'Listen. You go and tell Kenny we'll be in the coffee bar, then he can join us later.'

Phil smiled with delight and went off to the sports section while Kate and I found a table in the coffee bar.

'Honestly, Alison!' she said in exasperation as she ordered the coffees. 'I don't know what to make of you. Here's Phil, ready to do anything for you, and all you can do is treat him like dirt.'

I felt my face go hot. 'I don't treat him like dirt,' I protested. 'I honestly do want to get an early night.'

'Yes – and get in touch with Jeremy to tell him what time we'll be arriving tomorrow. If you think you can fool me . . . '

'Who's trying to fool you?'

'You are. Don't tell me you're not going to phone Jeremy as soon as you get home.'

'Of course I'm going to phone him. I told him I would. It would only be polite . . . '

'Huh! Come off it, Alison. There's more to it than that and you know it. Go on. Admit it.'

I scowled. She had me cornered. 'Anyone would think you didn't like him,' I muttered darkly.

Kate looked at me defiantly. 'As a matter of fact, I do. But all the same, I wouldn't trust him further than I could throw him.'

I leaned over the table. 'That's a horrible thing to say. If you don't take it back, I'll never speak to you again.'

Kate realized she'd gone too far. 'Oh, all right! I'm sorry. I shouldn't have said that. But I've told you before, I just don't want to see you hurt.'

I shook my head. 'You don't know Jeremy – not like

I do. If you did, you'd realize that's the last thing he'd ever do.'

But the look she gave me told me she wasn't convinced.

It was then that Phil arrived, followed shortly by Kenny. I was glad. If we had been left alone much longer Kate and I would have ended up at loggerheads. And the last thing in the world I wanted was for our friendship to come to an end.

We stayed there until half past nine when I glanced at my watch and saw what the time was.

'I really must go now!' I insisted. 'I've still got my case to pack.'

Kate remembered she hadn't packed hers either and thankfully made no further protest. We made our way home together until our ways parted and then Phil and I ambled the 400 yards to my house.

'All right if I come down tomorrow? I'd like to see you off, if you don't mind.'

'You don't have to, Phil.'

'I know I don't have to. I'd just like to, that's all. If you don't have any objection . . . '

'Of course I don't have any objection. Why should I?'

He gave a shrug of his broad shoulders and looked down at the ground. 'No reason . . . just that I have this feeling, that's all.'

'What feeling?'

'That you want us to finish.'

I was glad we were in the dark and that he couldn't see my face clearly. I felt my stomach go into a tight knot and a chill seep through my body. But once again I threw away the chance to be honest.

'Don't be ridiculous, Phil. Why should I want that to happen?'

'Like I said, no reason. But . . . ' he paused and looked deep into my eyes. 'But if you did, you'd be straight with me, wouldn't you? You'd tell me . . . '

I gulped and nodded, forcing a smile on to my lips. 'Of course, Phil. You know I would.'

I phoned Jeremy as soon as I arrived home. He must have been waiting because it only rang once before the receiver was picked up and I heard his voice.

'Hey! I've been waiting for you to phone all evening,' he said, his voice sending shivers running up and down my spine. 'Well, what are the arrangements?'

I told him what Mr Jarman had said.

'Great! I'll be there at half past three, just in case you get here early.'

But once again he couldn't speak for long.

'That's the trouble of having a doctor for a mother. Whenever she's on call, we have to go easy on the phone. See you tomorrow, Alison.'

My eyes misted over as I replaced the receiver. I sighed. There was less than twenty-four hours to go now.

I fell asleep dreaming of Jeremy, and when I awoke next morning to find the sunshine streaming through the thin summer curtains, I jumped out of bed and flung them open. Julie groaned and sank down further under the duvet.

'Do you have to do that?' she grumbled in a sleepy voice. 'Just you wait until you want to sleep in the mornings.'

But not even Julie could dispel the euphoria I felt at the thought of seeing Jeremy again. I just couldn't wait and constantly watched the clock.

'Oh, come on, Mum,' I complained for the tenth time in half an hour. 'We'll never get there if you don't hurry.'

She looked up from her coffee and shook her head. 'For goodness sake. It's not half past yet. It's only ten minutes away. You don't want to hang around outside, surely.'

I didn't care what I did. I just wanted to do something. Anything! I was so agitated that I couldn't sit still. Eventually, however, my mother condescended to put on her jacket and find the car keys and open the car boot so that I could put my case inside. She was so slow about everything that I wanted to scream with frustration.

What if the car won't start? I kept asking myself. What if there's a traffic jam in town? What if the car breaks down?

But the car did start. It didn't break down. And there was no traffic jam in the centre of town. Within ten minutes of leaving the house, we pulled into the leisure centre car park to discover that not only hadn't the minibus arrived, but that I was the first one there.

'There! I told you so,' she said disapprovingly.

Minutes later, Phil came driving in, having borrowed his father's car, and parked a few yards away. He waved and walked towards us, carrying some magazines and an even larger box of chocolates than last time.

'Thought you might like something to keep you busy on the journey,' he said with a grin that only accentuated his unhappiness.

I didn't know what to say. I mumbled my thanks and for about five minutes, we stood there awkwardly, my mother doing most of the talking, while all I could do was feel guilty. If only Phil wasn't so kind, I kept thinking, then I wouldn't feel so bad about meeting Jeremy again. But at last, the minibus and everybody else arrived and there was a frantic rush to get our luggage aboard so that we could get away.

Mum gave me a kiss and her usual veiled warning about taking care, while Phil quietly wished me a good weekend.

As the bus pulled away, I gave a final wave and sat back with a sigh of relief. We were on our way – at last.

That journey seemed to take ages. There were road-works along the motorways and I was filled with anxiety whenever we came to a halt behind a long tailback of cars and heavy lorries. But at last we arrived at the Leigh Delamere service area – only fifteen minutes later than Mr Jarman had expected. Instead of the hour stop that he had planned, he curtailed it to forty-five minutes, not that it worried me. The sooner we were on our way, the better. I was back on the bus five minutes before the others and soon we were ready to set off on the final stage of the journey.

'It'll be easier now,' he said over his shoulder as he drove out of the parking area. 'We'll be leaving the motorway soon and with a bit of luck, we'll avoid any more jams . . . '

It was exactly twelve minutes past four when I saw the signpost that stated we were entering Beckhaven: Beckhaven Welcomes Careful Drivers, it said. I sat forward in my seat and seconds later we came to the brow of a hill. In front of us was a clear blue sea with the sunshine glinting off the rippling waves. Then we rounded a bend and headed inland again for about half a mile before the road dipped steeply.

Then, suddenly, Beckhaven was below and in front of us. A small town nestling in the curve of a long bay with a small pier jutting into the sea; in the distance was a promontory dominated by a lighthouse.

My stomach turned several somersaults. We had arrived.

Chapter 13

Within minutes we were driving through the small seaside town and along the crowded promenade with a low sea wall separating it from the golden sands. It seemed so small in comparison with Grimborough; so small and so clean – and oh, so beautiful. My heart seemed to swell up inside me as I looked at it.

As the bus turned into the car park outside the town's swimming-pool, I looked for Jeremy, but there were so many people milling about I couldn't see anyone I knew.

Then I saw Damien and realized with a start that the guy he was talking to was Jeremy. My heart almost stopped beating and I felt so nervous that I wanted to run away. Mr Jarman parked the minibus in a vacant space, switched off the engine and turned round.

'Just a word before you go. We'll meet tomorrow

afternoon, after lunch. Don't be late. I'd like to leave before two o'clock if possible. Is that clear?' He looked around and when we'd nodded, went on. 'Very well. I'll see the competitors at Beck's Point tomorrow morning. The people you're staying with will take you there, so enjoy yourselves.'

Jeremy was standing outside the minibus, but though this was the moment I'd been longing for, I suddenly felt terribly nervous and shy.

I wondered if Kate was feeling the same way.

I don't know why I felt so self-conscious when I climbed off the bus but I do know it didn't last long. Jeremy took my case from me and as our hands met, his smile melted the embarrassed silence. Then he took my arm.

'Come on,' he said. 'Let's put your case in the car.'

As we moved towards it, I turned to catch a glimpse of Kate chatting happily with Damien, but Jeremy soon had my attention again.

'What do you think of it?' he asked proudly. 'Like it? Mum and Dad bought it for my eighteenth . . . '

I was so flabbergasted that all I could do was mumble my approval. All I was likely to get for my eighteenth birthday was a toy one. Not that Jeremy appeared to notice. He had found a mark on the gleaming red paintwork and was wiping it off with his handkerchief.

Instead of taking me immediately to his home, he showed me Beckhaven. We walked along the prom with its string of hotels, behind which was a wood-covered hill dotted with large private houses. As we strolled along, I felt as though I were in another world – a world where only the two of us existed – and I was dimly aware of the crowds that thronged the pavements.

Soon we were talking as though the long days that had separated us had never existed. We ambled hand in hand down to the sea and the incoming tide. A soft sea breeze wafted my hair and I felt so happy I could have stayed there all day.

We returned to the prom and a small café where Jeremy bought enormous ice creams and as we sat opposite each other eating them, our feet touched and became entwined, making me feel closer to him than ever.

'What have you been doing with yourself since Castell Brenin?' he asked.

I smiled coyly and shrugged my shoulders. 'Nothing much . . . and you?'

'Nothing much either. I've thought a lot about you though.'

I looked up, my eyes sparkling. 'Honestly?'

'Of course. I've thought of that last night when we went down to the lake.'

'So have I. And the time we went to the pub and got back late . . . '

He laughed. 'And Jan Webster gave you a ticking off . . . '

The memory made me giggle. 'That's right, and you and Damien left us in the lurch.'

He leaned across the table and placed his hand on mine. 'That was rotten, I know. Forgive me?'

His touch made me tingle and the way he looked at me, his dark eyes searching the very depths of my soul, made me feel weak all over.

'Don't be stupid!' I muttered hoarsely. 'Of course I

forgive you.'

Jeremy must have arranged with Damien for the four of us to go our separate ways and meet up later because they were waiting for us at the car park.

Jeremy's house was on the outskirts of Beckhaven. We drove along the western promenade before turning right up a winding, tree-lined lane with large detached houses set in spacious grounds on either side. We dropped off Kate and Damien and after promising to meet them later that evening, drove to the top of the hill to a large white house which overlooked the bay. It had a long drive, flanked by rhododendron bushes, which ended in a wide forecourt. It was only when he pulled up outside that I realized just how large his house was. It had a central doorway with Georgian windows and an oak door.

For the second time that day I began to feel nervous. It was like a palace, and I felt out of place.

'Jeremy! It's fantastic . . . ' I just stared at it.

'Yeah! It's not bad, is it?'

He said it so flippantly that I thought he must be joking, but when I glanced at him, I could see he was being perfectly serious. He just took it all for granted.

'Come on!' he said, when I stayed in the car, too scared to get out. 'Come and meet my mother.'

This was the part I'd been dreading. I felt sure I'd do something stupid. Jeremy led the way into a large hall which was bigger than our living room. The highly-polished parquet floor gleamed in the bright afternoon sunlight. He left my case at the foot of the stairs, grinned, took my hand and pulled me after him into the living room.

'Mum. This is Alison.' He ushered me into the centre

of a thickly carpeted room twice as long as it was wide and furnished with antiques.

His mother was sitting in a plush armchair near the window. She looked up when I entered, put down the magazine she'd been reading and came forward to greet me.

'Alison!' Her voice was warm and genuine. 'I'm so pleased to meet you. Jeremy's told me so much about you.'

Dr Sinclair was about forty-five and had the dark hair and eyes which Jeremy had inherited. He also had her fine features and unaffected smile.

'Did you have a good journey?'

She soon put me at ease and my fears disappeared. She asked if I'd like some coffee and when I offered to help, gladly accepted.

'That's very kind of you. It's not often I get an offer like that – not with two men about the house.' But before she took me to the kitchen, she turned to Jeremy. 'Don't think you're getting away without doing anything, my boy.' Her eyes twinkled as she spoke. 'You can take Alison's suitcase to her room, and then put your car into the garage. You know how your father feels about not finding a place to park when he gets home.'

Jeremy went off, grumbling good-naturedly that he was always being treated like a slave, while Dr Sinclair and I walked down a corridor at the side of the wide staircase until we arrived at the kitchen. 'Now perhaps we'll have a chance to get to know each other.'

Though there was very little to do apart from putting out the cups, just doing something made me feel more relaxed. Soon we were talking as though we had known each other for years instead of minutes, and I found out just where Jeremy got his charm and easy ways from.

'We'll have dinner later,' she said, glancing at her watch, 'as soon as Jeremy's father arrives home. Before then perhaps you'd like to see your room.'

Jeremy dutifully took me to my room and as he led me in, I gave a gasp of pleasure. It was at the side of the house, had two windows both of which looked out over the bay, and was big enough for four people at least.

Jeremy walked to the window and pointed to the lighthouse I'd noticed as we arrived.

'That's Beck's Point, where the race starts tomorrow morning.'

'Oh, yes! And who was Mr Beck when he was at home?'

Jeremy grinned and put his arm around my shoulder. 'His name was Sir Robert Beck and he lived in the sixteenth century. As a matter of fact, he owned all the land around here.'

'And gave Beckhaven its name?'

'Right first time. He had a large fortified mansion at Beck's Point, though it's only a ruin now.'

I gazed out over the bay.

'And where does it finish? The race, I mean.'

He pointed in the opposite direction. 'On the beach. Right in front of the swimming-pool.'

I frowned. 'Looks a long way.'

Jeremy laughed. 'Not as far as you think. It's three and a half miles.'

I was surprised. It appeared much longer than that. But the knowledge made me confident. Though I'd never swum in the sea before, nevertheless I'd swum that distance several times. I wondered if lake swimming was any different from swimming in salt water.

'Having second thoughts?' Jeremy asked.

I shook my head. 'Of course not. I was just wondering what it was going to be like, that's all.'

'No need to be worried. It's not that bad.'

'You've done it before?'

He nodded. 'Twice. Last year I came third. I think I have a good chance of winning this time.'

The way he said it made me look at him; there had been just a hint of sublime confidence in his voice that bordered on conceit. The thought flicked through my mind but no sooner had it registered than I thrust it away. Jeremy wasn't that kind of guy. And nobody, not even myself, was going to suggest it.

He left me a few moments later so that I could unpack, and told me to come down to the lounge when I was ready. It gave me a chance to look around as well as relax for a few minutes. It was a fantastic room, light and airy with pretty floral curtains at the windows, while the single bed was so comfortable it was sheer heaven just to lie on it.

But what pleased me most was the fact that I had it all to myself. For the first time in my life, I was going to sleep on my own with no kid sister to nag and annoy me. Suddenly, I was envious of Jeremy, and would have given the whole world to have his advantages for just one week.

Half an hour later, I had showered, unpacked and was stepping gingerly down the stairs. I knocked timidly at the door to the lounge and heard Jeremy's voice call me in.

He laughed when I closed the door behind me. 'You don't have to knock – just walk in. You're like one of the family while you're here. Come on – let me show you around. Dinner will be ready in about half an hour.'

There were even bigger grounds behind the house than in front. There was a large vegetable garden, a greenhouse filled with tomato plants and a small orchard of apple and pear trees. They even had a swimming-pool, not very large – perhaps half the size of a tennis court – but it was nevertheless a private swimming-pool, something I would have loved to have at home, except that it would have taken up most of our garden besides being completely out of place. I sat down by the side of it, dangling my fingers in the warm water. I felt as though I was in heaven. If only I could stay here for ever, I thought.

But that was before I met his father – or Selina.

Chapter 14

Dinner had been arranged for half past six, and though Jeremy's father had arrived home half an hour earlier from a business trip to London, I hadn't yet met him. He was in the lounge reading a newspaper when Jeremy took me in and introduced us. He was much older than Jeremy's mother, with dark hair receding from a broad forehead. He rose from the deep armchair to greet me and shook my hand firmly. 'It's nice to meet you . . . er . . . Alison,' he said, prompted by Jeremy. 'Did you have a good journey down?'

I told him I had and perched opposite him on the settee with Jeremy sitting by my side.

'Jeremy tells me you come from Grimborough,' he said, sipping a large whisky.

There was something in his manner that made me feel uneasy, and I nodded nervously. 'That's right.'

'It's near Birmingham, isn't it?'

'Yes, about twenty miles away.'

He frowned and pursed his lips. 'What's Birmingham like these days? Haven't been there for years.'

I told him about the Bullring and all the large department stores.

'Mmm!' he grunted. 'Can't say I'd fancy it very much. Can't stand these big cities. Can't get back quickly enough from London even.'

'I don't like them very much either,' I confessed, eager to agree. 'I much prefer Beckhaven.'

He looked at me over his spectacles. 'Wise girl! I don't suppose you'll be wanting to get back to Grimborough tomorrow, and I must say, I don't blame you.'

I don't think he meant to sound patronizing, but he made me feel as though he thought Grimborough was the grottiest place in the world. I know I'd often said it was, but when someone else did, it wasn't the same.

Jeremy must have sensed my annoyance.

'Oh, Dad! It can't be that bad. I rather fancy the sound of all those big shops. At least you'd feel that something's happening – not like Beckhaven.'

'Nonsense!' Mr Sinclair dismissed Jeremy's words with a mildly arrogant contempt, as though Jeremy didn't know what he was talking about. 'You wait until you see some of these places, my boy. Then you'll realize what a good place Beckhaven is.'

There it was again. The suggestion that anywhere else was inferior to Beckhaven. I felt that he was looking down on me as well as Grimborough and I didn't like it. I disagreed with Jeremy; I thought Beckhaven was a fabulous place, but I was angered by his father's remarks.

But before an argument could develop between Jeremy and his father, we were told that dinner was ready. I followed Mr Sinclair into the dining room. It faced the rear garden with the swimming-pool just a few yards from the open French windows. A breeze wafted the lace curtains – a breeze that cooled my temper.

Dinner was a very formal affair. The table was laid with so much cutlery that I didn't know which to use first. I'd heard that you started from the outside and worked in, but even so I took my cue from Jeremy and picked up the ones he used. His mother had prepared a fantastic meal, but that conversation with his father had made me feel awkward so that I hardly said anything while we ate.

There was wine on the table which Jeremy insisted on pouring out for me and once when I glanced up, he raised his glass with a wink of encouragement. His mother sensed that something was wrong too because she went out of her way to be pleasant to me.

But no matter what anyone did or said, I was convinced of one thing: I didn't like his father very much. He had made me feel as though I didn't belong.

After dinner, Jeremy suggested going down to the

'Captain's Cabin', a small fisherman's cottage which had been converted into a pub and was literally on the edge of the sea.

'You'll like it there. It's our haunt, though it'll probably be packed with holiday-makers.'

I didn't care where we went, just as long as I was with Jeremy. I slung my jacket over my shoulder and together we wandered down the drive and into the lane. Jeremy had phoned Damien before leaving and half way down we found him and Kate waiting for us.

'Isn't it fantastic?' breathed Kate when she was sure the boys couldn't hear. 'Damien actually has a tennis court in his garden – I couldn't believe it . . . '

'I know. Jeremy has a swimming-pool. Honestly, Kate. Doesn't it make you feel envious? Fancy living in a place like this all your life.'

Together we ambled down the meandering tree-lined lane and within fifteen minutes we were outside the 'Captain's Cabin'. As Jeremy had said, it couldn't have been nearer the sea; waves tumbled up the narrow stretch of sand and crashed against the huge rock on which it was built. He was also right about it being crowded. We squeezed into a small room, the walls of which were festooned with nets, glass floats and fishing tackle.

Someone in one corner called out to Jeremy and raised a hand.

'Over here. We've kept you a few places . . . '

That was an overstatement. We squeezed our way towards a crowd of people and discovered that there was hardly any room at all. But they edged up closer and managed to find enough room for the four of us to sit.

While Damien went to get some drinks, Jeremy made the introductions. There were eight people altogether and my mind was spinning so much with the noise and heat, I couldn't catch their names, except for one.

'This is Selina,' Jeremy shouted in my ear. 'Selina . . . Alison.'

I nodded at her and smiled. But all I got in return was a haughty stare as she looked me up and down, followed by a glimmer of a welcome. Then she went on talking to the guy called Ben who was pressed up against her and obviously enjoying it, which wasn't surprising.

Selina was slightly taller than me and wore a dazzlingly white sundress. She had long fair hair which gleamed in the soft lights and fell like a curtain of silk over her bare shoulders. She was one of the most beautiful girls I'd ever seen; she could easily have graced the cover of a glossy magazine, and I wondered what on earth she saw in the spotty guy she was with.

And then I knew. It was Jeremy she fancied.

I was talking to Jeremy when suddenly I had the feeling that someone was watching me, and glancing up, saw the look of sheer hatred in her eyes. And it was all directed at me.

But in an instant, it had vanished in a smile and all night I wondered if my eyes had been deceiving me.

Time was going to tell.

We arrived at the disco just after nine o'clock, and walked into a hall that pulsated to the heavy throb of music. There was so little room on the floor that Jeremy and I were pressed up close together as we moved to the intoxicating rhythms. Not that I minded

– I'd been looking forward to it all day.

Dancing with Jeremy was out of this world. Though we'd been together all afternoon, this was the nearest we'd been to each other and as we swayed to the gentle beat of a slow number and I closed my eyes, it was like being back at Castell Brenin all over again.

That evening flew far too quickly and the fact that we had to leave early because we were taking part in the swim next day didn't help.

But something happened half way through that upset me far more. When Jeremy went to get some more drinks, I'd gone to the cloakroom. When I returned I discovered that though the full glasses were on the table, there was no sign of him. Then I saw him, dancing with Selina. Though the room was dark, I could see them clearly enough in the pulsating coloured lights.

I felt jealousy tug at my heart.

But then I noticed that they were quarrelling. Selina was looking up at Jeremy and the expression on her face was angry and petulant. I obviously couldn't hear what they were saying, but I saw Jeremy's lips move and suddenly Selina stepped back, said something that must have been quite vicious, and stormed off the floor.

Thank goodness! Now perhaps he'll come back to me. Selina was much too beautiful for my liking.

But he didn't return. Instead he followed her across the dance floor to the exit. I saw him disappear through the swing doors.

For a moment, I didn't know what to do. Should I go after him and find out what had happened? Or should I stay where I was for him to return?

But I didn't trust Selina. Though I hadn't really spoken to her, the look she had given me in the 'Captain's Cabin' had been enough for me to dislike her.

So, promptly deciding that Jeremy was worth fighting for, I squeezed my way through the crowd.

When I pushed open the door, Selina and Jeremy were standing about ten yards away near the bend in the corridor. She had her hands on her hips and a determined look in her eyes, while Jeremy's stance told me he was just as furious with her.

I walked towards them.

'You're a fine one to accuse me of that,' I heard her say as I approached. 'I don't suppose you've ever . . . '

She broke off when suddenly she glanced in my direction and realized who I was. But Jeremy had his back to me now.

'It's your fault,' I heard him say. 'You're the one who let me down. If you hadn't . . . '

He was about to say something else, but Selina's attitude made him look over his shoulder. Neither said any more; Selina gave him a glare and stalked away without giving me so much as a second glance.

'What's the matter?' I asked, puzzled by what I'd overheard. 'I saw you leave and . . . '

'Everything's fine,' he snapped irritably. 'It was just . . . ' He paused and I could tell that he was trying to drum up an excuse. 'Selina had promised to do me a favour, and she let me down, that's all.'

Even though I was beginning to feel sick inside, I couldn't let the matter rest. 'Favour? What kind of favour?'

He shook his head, his lips in a straight line. 'It was nothing – nothing you should worry about.' Then he took a deep breath and ran a hand through his hair. 'Look! Do you mind if we go home? I think we both ought to have an early night if we're going to do well tomorrow.'

'Can't you tell me anything more than that?'

'Alison! Just drop it, okay?'

Immediately he apologized. 'I'm sorry, I shouldn't have spoken to you like that . . . but that Selina – she's nothing but trouble . . . '

As if I didn't know!

Chapter 15

I slept late the following morning and it was Jeremy, bringing me a mug of steaming coffee, who woke me with a gentle shake of my shoulder. I started out of my sleep and remembered that I'd been dreaming of Selina – a dream in which we'd been rivals for Jeremy, a recollection that reminded me all too clearly of last night.

Jeremy pulled aside the curtains and looked out towards Beck's Point. 'We couldn't have a better day – the sea's like a millpond, hardly a swell.' He turned and gave me a grin that made all my fears about Selina seem groundless. 'Better not be too long. Mum's preparing a light breakfast. Should be ready in about twenty minutes.'

After he left, I crossed the thickly carpeted room and peered out. The sea really did look calm, though Beck's

Point seemed further away than ever and apprehension tugged inside me. I was down in the kitchen in just a quarter of an hour and as we had breakfast, Jeremy explained the strategy of the swim.

'We start at low tide, when the tide's almost non-existent. That makes the going easier as we swim out into the bay.'

'Don't we make for Beckhaven beach?' I asked, slightly perplexed.

He shook his head. 'No. By swimming out into the centre of the bay we can take advantage of the tide when it turns, then all we have to do is follow our canoeist and with a bit of luck, strike land just in front of the lido.'

He made it sound so easy, yet I knew from experience that so many things could happen in the water. By the time we arrived at the lighthouse quite a crowd had gathered. Some had wandered on to the beach, the sand hard and damp, to encourage those competitors who were limbering up, but most were sitting on the grassy stretch immediately above the rocks.

Though it was early, the air was warm and since it was now approaching ten o'clock – the time the race had been scheduled to begin – I slipped off my track suit and smeared myself with lanolin before nervously joining Jeremy in the trek down to the shore. A group of officials were gathered there, including the mayor who was to start the race.

I discovered that Damien had volunteered to act as my canoeist, while Selina, to my consternation, had chosen to accompany Jeremy.

Presently, the chief steward asked us to gather round.

'I'd better explain the procedure for the benefit of those who haven't competed before. I want the canoeists to follow the rescue boat,' he said, pointing to a blue boat anchored a couple of hundred yards offshore. 'And of course, I want you swimmers to keep an eye on your canoeist. And if you get into any difficulty, don't hesitate . . . it could be dangerous. Just tell your canoeist what's wrong and hang on until the rescue boat comes to get you.' He looked around at us all. 'Now, if you're all ready, would you please wade up to waist height, form a straight line and keep your eye on the starter. Then it's up to you, Mr Mayor,' he said with a grin.

We waded dutifully up to our waists and satisfying ourselves that we had formed a straight line, turned to face the bay. Our canoeists were just a few yards ahead of us, waiting. I watched the mayor raise his flag. He kept it above his head for a few seconds and then brought it down. I pushed myself forward into the gentle swell – the race had begun.

I found it strange at first. This was the first time I'd ever swum a long distance in the sea; lakes had been my biggest experience up till then. Though warmer than Witham Water, the swell took me some time to get used to. What had appeared flat and smooth from Jeremy's house, was actually a gentle roll. And in those first crucial minutes, the troughs put me off my stroke so that I began to trail.

But gradually, when I got the hang of it, I began to plough strongly through the water and I noticed Damien turn round in surprise when I caught up with him, so that he had to increase his stroke. From there on, I was aware of only two things: the canoe in front of me and the way my body was adjusting to the buoyancy of the water. Before long, my body heated up with the exertion so I was hardly aware of the threatening chill of the water. My breathing became regular and I knew that all the months of practice in the swimming-pool at Grimborough had been worthwhile.

Mr Jarman had warned me so often of the psychological danger of boredom, so I thought of all the most pleasurable things in my life. Which at that time, of course, meant Jeremy. I allowed my mind to wander and dreamt of living in Beckhaven and seeing him every day – a thought that made my whole body glow with satisfaction.

I wasn't even aware of the other swimmers – not even one hour and thirty-six minutes later when my fingers scraped sand and I was trudging up the shore to the reception committee on the beach.

It was Kate who came rushing down to meet me.

'Alison! You've done it . . . you've done it . . . !' She didn't seem to mind that she was up to her knees in the water and that her jeans were getting wet. In fact, I only dimly realized it myself – I was so exhausted – as it crossed my mind how ridiculously she was behaving. Then her words gradually sank in.

'You've won! she was shouting. 'Alison! You've won . . .'

I couldn't believe it. Glancing round, I discovered to my surprise that I was the only swimmer on the beach. I had come in before everybody, even the men. Someone – it must have been Jeremy's mother – threw a towel over my shoulders and congratulated me. My mind was spinning as I waited for the other competitors to arrive. I didn't have to wait long. Within a minute, the next swimmer came trudging through the surf; it was Ben, the guy who had been drooling over Selina the previous evening, and Mr Jarman, who had joined the crowd of well-wishers, told me what I should do.

I gave Ben a welcoming handshake and then stood, oblivious to my shivering body, anxiously scanning the other swimmers as they arrived. But there was no sign of Jeremy. I felt my stomach twist inside me as I thought the worst. And then I saw him.

The rescue boat came zooming on to the beach with Jeremy sitting dejectedly inside. It glided up the sloping sand and as he got out, I noticed him limping slightly. I ran towards him, realizing what had happened. He'd had cramp and had to withdraw from the race.

'Oh, Jeremy!' I said. 'I'm so sorry . . . '

But that's all I managed to say as he brushed past me and stormed up the beach. I stared after him, unable to believe, let alone understand, why he was treating me so callously.

I saw his mother hand him his towel. He didn't say anything to her either. He just strode towards the lido and the changing rooms.

I ran after him; I wanted to plead with him not to be so disappointed, to assure him that there was always next year. He was certain to win then. But before I could reach him, he had disappeared into the men's changing rooms.

Half an hour later, we returned to the beach where the awards ceremony was to take place, but though I searched the crowds for Jeremy, there was no sign of him.

'And now ladies and gentlemen,' the chief steward

announced, 'I shall ask our Mayor, Councillor Merriweather, to present the trophies to the winning contestants.'

They were announced in reverse order, ladies first. Two older women went forward first to receive small cups and certificates, but before he called me, the chief steward made another announcement.

'Before I call on the outright winner of the race to come forward to receive her trophy,' his voice boomed over the beach, 'there is something special I'd like to say. This young lady is only sixteen. She has only been swimming long distances for a short time, so her trainer tells me . . . ' – he smiled and looked down at Mr Jarman – 'though I find that rather hard to believe. This young lady came first overall, before any of the men even. But not only that – she has broken the record for the Beckhaven Bay Annual Swim.'

An excited murmur broke out and several hands clapped me on my back, not that I noticed much; I was too confused both by the fact that I'd come in first and by Jeremy's behaviour. To be told that I'd broken the record as well . . .

Then he called me up. 'Ladies and gentlemen, I call on Miss Alison Anderson to come to the rostrum.'

My head was in a whirl as I went to meet the Mayor and the applause thundered in my ears. He shook my hand, said something I was too bemused to understand even if I could have heard him, and handed me a large trophy and a certificate. As I returned to the others Kate threw her arms around me while Mr Jarman looked as though he'd won the race himself.

'Your father should be here,' he said. 'I know how proud he would be.'

But I was too concerned about Jeremy to give more than a brief thanks. As the men's awards were presented, I glanced around for Jeremy, hoping against hope that he'd returned, but I couldn't see him anywhere. He certainly wasn't with his mother who was also anxiously scanning the crowds.

I did notice, however, that one other person was missing – Selina – and I had a sudden sinking feeling in the pit of my stomach that she was with him.

We all trooped over to the restaurant above the lido where a lunch had been arranged for us before we left for home. He didn't turn up there either, even though all the contestants had been invited. There was just an empty place next to Damien who, curiously, couldn't or wouldn't look at me. And then I noticed another empty place. It was next to Ben.

I realized with a girl's quick intuition that it belonged to Selina.

Chapter 16

That lunch tasted like sawdust in my mouth. Though it was expertly cooked and beautifully presented, I was so upset by Jeremy's behaviour that I had no appetite at all. I sat next to the Mayor and what he must have thought of me, I'll never know. Though he spoke to me, I was silent and preoccupied, thinking only of Jeremy and why he was treating me this way. I hadn't done anything to him. It wasn't my fault that he'd developed cramp when he was within sight of the shore. It wasn't my fault that he'd had to withdraw from the race. So why was he treating me like this – as though he blamed me for something beyond my control?

Eventually, after about an hour, it was all over. The final speeches had been said, I'd been congratulated once again, and all the competitors, officials and participants were thanked and wished a safe and pleasant journey home.

When I joined the others outside, I realized that I couldn't journey home immediately. My suitcase was still at Jeremy's house.

I told Mr Jarman about my plight.

He glanced anxiously at his watch. 'Well, we'll have to leave soon – in half an hour at the latest – if we're to get home as arranged. We don't want your mother panicking when you don't get back in time, do we?' He thought for a moment. 'Tell you what. We'll wait for the others to get here and then I'll drive you to Jeremy's house.'

But that didn't suit my purposes at all. I desperately needed to talk to Jeremy in private before leaving to find out what had gone wrong; having everyone waiting outside in the minibus, urging me to hurry, was the last thing I wanted.

It was Damien who solved my problem by offering to drive me there. He had borrowed his father's car for the morning.

'Come on! We won't be long.' He led the way to his car, accompanied by a worried Kate. 'I'll get you back in time.'

But though my case was packed and waiting at the

foot of the stairs, I doubted very much whether he would. So, with Kate sitting next to him in the front and me perched anxiously on the back seat, he drove swiftly along the promenade and up the hill.

Jeremy's mother was getting into her car when we arrived. She seemed relieved when she saw me, yet there was worry and anxiety in her eyes too, mixed, I thought, with a trace of embarrassment.

'I was just about to come down and get you,' she explained. 'I was worried when you didn't arrive.'

While she was telling Damien not to wait, that she would drive me down, I glanced into the garage. Jeremy's car was no longer there. She noticed my glance as she returned.

'I'm glad we're on our own,' she said. 'I wanted to talk to you . . . to explain.'

Her words had such an ominous ring that I almost burst into tears on the spot.

She led me into the lounge and asked me to sit down. She sat opposite me but before she could begin, I asked the question that had been plaguing me.

'Where's Jeremy?' My voice was a tight hoarse whisper and though I wanted to know the truth, I dreaded the answer. 'Where has he gone?'

She looked down at the floor, biting her lip. Then she looked up and gave a wan smile.

'It's about Jeremy I wanted to talk to you,' she began, deliberately ignoring my question. 'And Selina.'

There was a tightness in my throat. 'Selina? What about Selina?'

'Did he mention her when you first met at Castell Brenin? Did he tell you about her?'

I shook my head. I blinked furiously to hold back the

tears as a lump hardened in my throat.

She took a deep breath. 'Then I had better tell you, hadn't I?' She came over, sat next to me on the huge settee and took my hand. 'It's like this. Jeremy and Selina . . . well . . . they've known each other since they were children, and over the last year . . . they've become very friendly.'

'You mean she's his girlfriend?'

'Yes, at least she was until a fortnight ago. They quarrelled the night before he left for that swimming course, and when he came back, he found she was going out with Ben. Have you met Ben?'

'Yes.' My voice sounded as though it was coming from a faraway place; as though it didn't belong to me at all. I remembered the way Selina had looked at me in the pub, and the way she had held on so possessively to Ben. Now I knew why it hadn't added up. She had been deliberately trying to make Jeremy envious, which explained that look of sheer hatred she'd given me.

Then Dr Sinclair confirmed my suspicions. 'She was trying to make Jeremy jealous,' she continued. 'At least, that's what I believe. And . . . please forgive me for saying this, Alison . . . I think she succeeded.'

I recalled that angry scene with Selina outside the disco and the pathetic excuse Jeremy had made. It all fitted together. Anger flared up inside me, burning my cheeks and clouding my eyes.

'Where is he now?' I asked, knowing the answer even before his mother told me.

'He's gone out,' she said hesitantly, 'in his car.'

'With Selina?'

She nodded, 'I'm afraid so.'

I shook my head and turned away so that she

couldn't see my tears. Then I felt a hand on my shoulder.

'I am sorry about this, Alison,' she said sympathetically. 'I really am annoyed with Jeremy. I warned him he shouldn't treat you like this. And that incident this morning when he wouldn't even speak to you . . . I think he was angry because you had come first and he hadn't completed the course. That was both childish and unforgivable – and I shall tell him so.' Her eyes had a faraway look as she sighed. 'Perhaps we're to blame – his father and I. We have rather spoilt him, I'm afraid.'

I was so angry that I couldn't even listen to her and instinctively I shook her hand away. For a moment or two there was silence until an old grandfather clock in the corner chimed the half hour.

Then she spoke. 'I don't want to hurry you, Alison. But the time's getting on and the bus will be waiting for you.'

I glanced round. 'But I must see Jeremy before I go,' I cried desperately. 'Isn't he coming back to say goodbye to me?'

She frowned and shook her head again. 'No,' she said sadly, and added, 'But he did ask me to tell you that he'd phone – to explain – I shall make sure he does.'

I thought for a moment. He didn't have the courage or the decency to tell me to my face, so why should I bother to listen to his excuses over the phone? The reason for his behaviour was plain; his pride was such that he couldn't take being beaten by a mere girl. But more than that, and even more hurtful to me, he preferred Selina, and that's all there was to it.

'No!' I said firmly, making a sudden decision. 'Please tell him not to. Tell him that I'd rather he didn't . . . that I understand . . . '

We were ten minutes late when Dr Sinclair drove me down to the car park on the sea front. But during that short journey, my mind went over all he had said to me; I recalled his words of love when we sat in the moonlight at the side of the lake at Castell Brenin. They were meaningless. Even as he uttered them, he must have been thinking of Selina, and I couldn't help wondering if when he had invited me to stay, he had been using me just as Selina had used Ben.

The thought made me boil. How dare he use me that way? How dare he treat me as a stopgap! Just someone to fill in the time until another girl came along.

But even as I thought, my cheeks began to burn. My mother's accusations came flooding into my mind and I realized that I had behaved just as badly.

I felt shame well up inside me. I had used Phil just as callously and brazenly as Jeremy had used me. Phil had been hurt too – just as I had been hurt. That much had been obvious, and now I knew exactly how he must have felt. But in spite of my treatment of him, he had been kind. He had brought me presents, had waved me goodbye when I left Grimborough, while all I could do was moon over Jeremy.

I felt nothing but guilt and humiliation as Dr Sinclair pulled into the car park just a few yards from the minibus and came to a halt. Mr Jarman was at the door, glancing around and gave a sigh of relief when he saw us.

She switched off the engine and turned to me. 'Before you go, Alison. Do you mind if I ask you something? Something personal?'

I looked at her warily. 'What?'

'I was wondering if you had someone waiting for you back at Grimborough.'

It was as though she had been reading my thoughts, and for a moment I was so shocked that I hesitated.

'Yes . . . yes, I do . . . and I haven't treated him very nicely either. But how did you know?'

'Simple! You're a very pretty girl. There just had to be a boy at home who was keen on you.' Then she squeezed my hand. 'Be nice to him, dear. I have the feeling he deserves it.'

She walked me to the minibus. 'I hope you have a good journey home and thank you for coming. It was nice having you stay.'

'Thank you for having me,' I whispered, trying hard not to cry. I was about to say that I had enjoyed it, but it just wasn't true, not any more.

'And if you'd like to phone me any time, you know you can,' she added.

'Yes! Yes, I will!' I promised.

But as the minibus drew away and we waved to each other, we both knew that I wouldn't.

Chapter 17

I sat next to Kate feeling depressed and bitter. I recalled that for the second time in just over a week, I was leaving Jeremy in tears. But this time it was so different.

Leaving him at Castell Brenin meant leaving him with some kind of hope that we would meet again in the future and carry on from where we had left off. But this time it was final. There was no going back. There was no hope at all.

I turned my head away and stared blindly out of the window, trying to keep my tears from Kate who was talking away, pretending that nothing had happened. I wasn't listening to her; all I did was utter the occasional grunt to keep her happy and convey the impression that I heard all she was saying.

I gave a sigh and recalled the events of the weekend. I had expected so much when I arrived on Saturday afternoon and now just twenty-four hours later, not only had my hopes and aspirations been dashed into tiny pieces, but my pride had been hurt too.

There had been Jeremy's father and his incessant questioning and the feeling that he was looking down on me for living in a town like Grimborough. Though to be fair to him, he had always been polite; he hadn't really said anything insulting. It was just my reaction to what had been left unsaid.

And there had been the evening at the disco when the antagonistic vibes from Selina had worried me, destroying my confidence, and making me feel as though I didn't belong. I had dismissed them at the time as being a mere figment of my imagination, though their effect had been real enough. But my first impression had proved right. There had been that air of embarrassment making me feel the odd one out. But then, I had to admit, it was reasonable and understandable. After all, their friends knew something that I didn't; they knew that Jeremy and Selina had been going steady for some time, and my appearance must have surprised them. I could imagine the girls closing ranks against me, the intruder, and protecting Selina with their sympathy.

As if Selina needed protecting, I said to myself with bitterness; Selina knew exactly how to look after herself – and how to get exactly what she wanted. After all, she had got Jeremy, hadn't she?

A hand placed on my arm made me turn. Kate was smiling gently at me, and I realized that she too was trying to protect me in her own way.

'You haven't told me . . . ' Her voice was soft and comforting. 'Did you see Jeremy before leaving?'

I shook my head. 'He'd gone out.' I paused, wondering whether or not I should tell her all that his mother had revealed. In spite of the humiliation, I needed to confide in somebody. 'Oh, Kate. I've been such a fool. When I went inside, I found he'd gone out – with Selina . . . after all he'd said to me at Castell Brenin. And I believed every word. It was Selina he loved all the time . . . '

'I know,' she said quietly. 'At least, that it was a possibility.'

'How could you possibly know?' I exclaimed.

'Surely that's obvious. Damien told me. He told me about her at Castell Brenin.'

'And you never told me?' Steve Lawson, who was sitting in front of us, half turned his head so I lowered my voice. 'You should have.'

'But I tried to, Alison. I warned you about him – don't you remember? Though I said I liked him, I told you that I wouldn't trust him further than I could throw him. Besides, I couldn't tell you everything . . .

I'd promised Damien I wouldn't.'

I sat back and folded my arms angrily. 'You should have. I'm your best friend . . . at least, I thought I was.'

'Oh, Alison! Of course you are. Anyway, Damien told me that it was all over between Selina and Jeremy, so perhaps he meant all he told you . . . '

I shook my head. 'No. If he had, he wouldn't have treated me like he has. I wouldn't have done that to him.'

'No!' she conceded. 'But then your parents haven't spoilt you as his have . . . '

That's what his mother had said, and her observation startled me because deep down that's what I had thought too. I'd thought it briefly when he told me he'd been given a brand new car for his eighteenth birthday, but I'd ignored it at the time.

'And I suppose it explains his behaviour this morning when he came in on the rescue boat and stormed off. You'd beaten him.'

That's what I'd thought earlier, but now that I'd had time to reflect, I realized that it could have been sheer anger on my part.

'That's because he had cramp . . . he was so disappointed.' I was still prepared to defend him in spite of all that had happened.

She shook her head decisively. 'You were ahead of him, long before he caught cramp and had to withdraw – I could see. Damien lent me his binoculars . . . I could see him following Selina in her canoe.'

I frowned as I looked at her. I was learning something new every minute. 'Honestly?'

'Yes, honestly. You were ahead of him and perhaps he knew it. But even if he didn't then, he knew it later and couldn't accept the fact that you were a better long-distance swimmer than he was. Honestly, Alison, he isn't worth crying over. Phil's a much nicer guy.'

She was so right. The way he treated me had proved that, and I had been too blind to appreciate it.

'I know, Kate,' I said with a sigh. 'Thank goodness, he doesn't know how I felt about Jeremy. He'd be . . . '

Something about Kate's attitude made me pause; her body had stiffened at my words and her lips were tight.

'What is it, Kate?' I said, and then seeing the look in her eyes guessed the worst.

'Oh, Alison.' Her voice quivered a little. 'But he does know! You see, I told him . . . '

My heart stood still. 'Oh, you haven't!' I cried. 'But when . . . why?'

'Friday night . . . after he took you home. Phil came running down our street as Kenny and I were saying goodnight. He said he wanted to talk to me, and when he asked me about Jeremy, I just didn't know what to say . . . ' She gave a helpless shrug of the shoulders.'I couldn't lie to him.'

'You could have told him that you didn't know anything,' I muttered bitterly.

'How could I? He gave me the impression that he knew everything. So I told him that you'd fallen for Jeremy . . . and that I thought it was only a temporary crush.'

I remembered the sad expression in his eyes when he came to wave goodbye. He knew even then – and yet he had bought me those magazines and chocolates.

'Oh, Kate!' I sighed. 'What am I going to do? What's he going to think of me?'

She shook her head slowly. 'You should have told him the truth, shouldn't you? Then he could have made a decision for himself.' Then she added. 'Perhaps he already has.'

Her words made me go cold. I was beginning to realize that what I felt for Jeremy must have been a ridiculous infatuation, and as Kate had predicted, only now that I might have lost Phil did I appreciate what he meant to me. Already I regretted the shameful way I'd treated him.

The rest of the journey dragged and I felt so dejected that all I could do was sit and mope and scold myself for having been so stupid. If only I could turn the clock back, I kept saying over and over to myself; I wouldn't be so foolish again.

But miracles never happen. At least, not to me.

As our minibus pulled into the lido car park, my eyes scanned the line of cars for a sight of my mother. I desperately wanted to talk to her, to tell her all that had happened. She always knew how to console me; she always managed to make me feel that things would get better. But there was no sign of her.

Phil was there though. He stood on the steps at the entrance to the leisure centre and when he saw our minibus, he strode purposefully towards it. My heart was in my mouth. I saw the grim expression on his face and knew what he was about to do. He was going to give me a piece of his mind – tell me exactly what he thought of me and that it was all over. I couldn't find it in my heart to blame him.

I deserved all I was going to get.

'Oh, Kate!' I said, my voice trembling. 'What am I going to do?

Phil didn't smile when I stepped off the minibus. He just took my case.

'Your mother couldn't make it,' he said sternly. 'She

asked me to pick you up, so I borrowed my father's car.'

I could hardly look at him.

'Which is just as well,' he went on, 'because I wanted to speak to you . . . alone.'

He took my arm and led me to his car. He opened the door without a word, slung my case on to the back seat and stood aside to let me get in. He closed the door and walking round the front of the car, let himself into the driver's side. I trembled as I watched him.

He didn't turn on the engine. He just turned to me instead.

'Okay, Alison! I think I've taken all I can from you. I want to know where I stand.'

I couldn't say a word. My mouth felt as though it was full of sand and my throat was so dry that all I could do was gulp.

'I'm waiting,' he went on when I didn't reply. 'I want to know about this Jeremy guy . . . I mean it. It's either him or me.'

Tears began to stream down my cheeks; tears of shame and humiliation that made me choke with embarrassment. But Phil didn't move; he made no attempt to console me.

'It's no use behaving like this, Alison. I don't want to hurt you, but you've hurt me – terribly – over the past few weeks. Like I said, I want to know where I stand.'

I wiped my eyes with the back of my hand. 'Oh, Phil!' I sniffed back the tears. 'I know I've treated you terribly, and I'm sorry . . . '

'You don't have to tell me that . . . I'm only too aware of it already!' he insisted. 'I'm not kidding, Alison . . . it's either Jeremy or me . . . you can't expect to have it both ways . . . '

'I don't!' I protested. 'Honestly I don't. But as far as Jeremy is concerned – if you must know – it's all over . . . '

Phil frowned, the doubt showing in his eyes. 'You don't really expect me to believe that.'

'But it's true!' The words came out sharply, but the anger was directed at myself, not him. 'I've been a fool . . . I realize that now. And I have treated you badly. Please, Phil . . . please forgive me . . . '

Tears began to blur my eyes once more, but this time an arm crept round my shoulder and pulled me towards him. I buried my head against him.

'That's all I wanted to know,' he said, and when I looked up, I saw a smile light up his eyes. 'So . . . perhaps I'd better get you home, hadn't I? Your mother'll be worried – wondering where you are.' He gave a grin. 'Perhaps she thinks I've kidnapped you . . . '

He switched on the engine and pulled away. 'By the way,' he said as he drove home. 'That gig I told you about . . . next week.'

'With Double Trouble?'

He nodded. 'That's right. Do you still want to go?'

Did I want to go? It was what I wanted more than anything in the whole world at that moment.

'Oh, yes, Phil, I really do!' I breathed.

He glanced briefly and grinned. 'The gig it is, then. Double Trouble, here we come!'

I sat back in my seat and smiled contentedly. Things were getting better every second. And I remembered what my mother had told me so often : things are never as good – or as bad – as you think they are.

But she was wrong. At this moment, they were perfect!